THE PRINCESS KNIGHT

A FANTASY STORY WITH REAL LIFE STAKES

C.H. SMITH

The characters and events portrayed in this book are fictitious. Any similarity to real persons, living or dead, is coincidental and not intended by the author.

Copyright © 2023 C. H. Smith. All rights reserved

No part of this book may be reproduced, or stored in a retrieval system, or transmitted in any form or by any means, electronic, mechanical, photocopying, recording, or otherwise, without express written permission of the publisher.

Published by Swamp Island Words

ISBN: 979-8-9877795-1-4

Printed in the United States of America

In memory of all the children gone too soon.

For all the parents who live on anyway.

N
LAMOORE
HOUSTONIA

RED
DRAGON
SEASCAPE
The Kingdom of
CRYSTAL FORGE

Contents

Chapter 1

I am not exactly sure what answer I was expecting from the quiet, bearded guy a few stools down from me at the bar, but I was definitely not prepared for the one he provided. I had half-expected him to brush me off or offer some noncommittal response. If he was more liquored-up than I had thought, I might have heard a rant about an ex-wife or cheating girlfriend. If he was piss drunk, I would have expected pitiful whining about missed opportunities and regret. His answer did not match any of those.

"How's it going, big fella?" I asked out of boredom.

He looked at me with the wide eyes of a child just caught sneaking into his dad's locked office to peek at something he knew was off limits.

"My princess is gone, and I miss her." Then after a long pause, he continued, "Sometimes, lately, I struggle to remember her face perfectly. And the joy of her laugh, I remember, but not the tone or sound, just the feeling it caused. That's not always enough."

I am a fairly well-read guy for a bar rat and have never met a stranger. In that moment, however, I was at a loss for words. So, I did the only logical thing possible.

"Brandee? Another round for me and my friend," I said, buying some time to collect my thoughts. There is an unspoken rule between most bar patrons. Conversations must pause in front of the bartender, unless said bartender was previously involved, or her opinion would add value in the conversation. The bearded man that had been nursing his beer did not honor the sacred tradition.

"I don't even know why I'm here. I don't drink much anymore, but I couldn't think of anywhere else to be," he said, draining his warm beer and accepting a new one from Brandee.

"Well, I think this is a fine place to be. A few drinks, good conversation, food that won't kill ya," I said with a laugh. "Mighty fine place to be."

The man just nodded and sipped his beer. I thought that was the end of it, so I asked Brandee about her studies.

"Pretty good, Jake," she said as she perched on the bar in front of a large, open history book. "But I do have an exam tomorrow morning, so if I'm a little slow on the pour, just holler."

Again, boredom got the best of me. I slid over a couple seats next to the bearded man.

"What'd you say your name was?"

"I didn't, but it's Daniel."

"I'm Jake. Don't think I've ever seen you in here before," I continued, trying to get the conversational ball rolling.

"Nope," Daniel replied, reaching for his wallet.

"Don't be in a hurry, friend. The old couple at the end there are boring, and I'm too old to hang with the college crowd. But me and you, that's just about right," I said.

This guy had something to get off his chest, I could tell. Daniel paused and looked around the bar. Then he sighed and settled back onto his stool.

"There, that's better. Now, what you do for a living, Daniel?"

"I'm an out-of-work school teacher," he said.

"That's hard. Raising other people's kids, I mean," I told him. "I'm a car salesman, and sales have been good. Let me buy you another beer."

"Maybe after this one is done," Daniel said quietly. "Not sure I'll be up for another one."

"Sure you will be," I said with a smile and took a sip. "What subject did you teach?"

Daniel did not respond right away; instead, he stared at the watch on his wrist. "Subject? High school history."

"One of my favorites! At least better than English lit. Having to read a bunch of stories that didn't make a hoot of sense, written by a bunch of dead folks, never appealed to me," I said honestly, shrugging my shoulders.

"Stories are powerful, though. At least the good ones are, anyway," he said, a vacant look still in his eyes.

I realized I was getting back into strange territory, but now I had to know what haunted him. What made him talk about princesses and powerful stories?

"Do you know any stories like that? Stories with power?" I asked. Daniel nodded, so I pushed on. "We have time. Tell me one."

"I'm not sure about that. The last story I told didn't end well for anybody," he replied.

"Was it about the princess you spoke of earlier?" I asked. My fingers tightened on my glass as I watched for a reaction.

The large, bearded man lifted his head to look me in the eyes. "It was a story I told my daughter, Josie, and yes, it was about the princess I mentioned." I noticed his eyes showed a yearning for something, but I was not sure if it was to tell the story or to forget it.

"I'd hear it if you'd tell it," I said.

"It's not a story I've ever told anyone but her," he said quietly. "And I don't think this is the place or the time."

I watched the enormous struggle happen within him. Daniel's fist clenched tightly, and small beads of sweat appeared on his forehead. The yearning intensified till it burned through him. He needed to tell the story again. He needed it to be heard.

"There is never the perfect time or place for anything," I said, leaning in closer. "There is only now, on that barstool, in this bar. Tell your story. It'll be better than the ending of this massacre of a football game on the TV."

Daniel's shoulders relaxed as he polished off his beer. The intense look in his eyes was replaced with the far-away gaze of a man lost in a memory. A memory replayed so often it was comfortable and inviting between the painful edges.

"Alright, but first, I'll take you up on that next beer," he said.

Chapter 2

A long time ago in a land far, far away – or, if you prefer, *Once upon a time* – there was a kingdom known as Crystal Forge. It was a large kingdom, filled with beautiful and wondrous things. Unimaginably tall waterfalls filled crystal-clear pools that fed tranquil streams. Soaring trees in lush green forests were home to abundant wildlife. The cities were regal and pristine each encircled by fertile farmland. To the south, the coast was lined with pink, sandy beaches and blue water. To the north and east, the Dragon Spine Mountains offered protection and unspoiled beauty. Finally, to the west was the Endless Sea of Grass, known as much for its fertile soil as its vastness.

Crystal Forge was a truly beautiful place. It was also quite magical. It was home to the Elves of the Golden Age. The only known colony of water sprites inhabited the two major rivers. Sirens swam in the bay to the south, and dragons soared over the mountains. Even commonplace animals such as deer or squirrels had a touch of magic. Some lived much longer than would be considered natural, others seemed to possess higher levels of intelligence. Though they were rarer, some of the animals could talk! Crystal Forge was both wondrous and mystical. Light causes shadow, as they say, and there was darkness in the Forge as well. This is a tale of one child's quest to fight against that darkness. To fight it at all costs.

There were many castles in the Forge, but only the three oldest are worth mentioning. The blood-red castle at the base of the Dragon Spine Mountains was said to have been built by the dragon riders of lore. The white sandstone castle on the edge of the grass sea was low and sprawling, and was almost as old as the Red Dragon Castle. Then there was Seascape Castle on the southern coast. It was the newest of the major castles, although no one could remember anyone who would have seen the castle when it was built. Seascape Castle, which was made entirely of coral rock, was home to the Queen, the Princess, and one big brown Shaggy Dog.

Princess Sophia loved to walk the sandy pink beach just below the castle in search of perfect seashells. The perfect shell did not have to be really big, nor did it have to be extremely small. It did not have to be pure white or wildly colored. It did not have to be round or oblong. It could be any of these things or none of them. It just needed to be perfect. The Princess could think of no better way to spend her birthday morning. She loved being on the beach or in the Queen's forest or even the drill yard, as long as she was outside. She felt free and alive, or perhaps merely unencumbered by layers of cloth and frilly lace daily life in the castle required. With her dark hair blowing across her face, she gazed over the sea longingly before turning back to the castle. It was time for her birthday celebration complete with cake and ice cream, but also with dresses and ceremony and oh so many people.

On her way across the short dunes but before the climb up the bluff, the Princess was joined by a big, fluffy brown dog. The dog, which closely resembled a small bear, had long, unruly hair, each strand of which seemed to want to lay in any direction but that of the hair around it. He had a sort of bumbling energy that some might confuse with clumsiness or dimness. Shaggy Dog was far from either of these things, though. In fact, he was one of the animals in the Forge that could talk, although he did so rarely and even then usually only to the Princess.

As he lumbered towards her, the Princess giggled, and her light blues eyes sparkled. Shaggy Dog jumped up eager to embrace the Princess. On his hind legs, Shaggy Dog towered over the Princess as he placed his paws on her shoulders. Hair and laughter were everywhere as these two friends reveled in just being together.

"Shaggy Dog! I am so happy to see you," exclaimed the Princess once her laughter had subsided. Even if Shaggy Dog had wanted to deny how happy he felt, his boat-paddle tail gave him away, swishing feverishly from side to side. "I'm so glad you came. Are you coming to the castle?" pleaded the Princess. "The party will be awfully dull, but better with you there."

Shaggy Dog's head lowered and the motion of his tail slowed as he muttered, "I'm sure the Queen won't be thrilled, but for you, Princess... anything."

"Oh, thank you! Thank you! This party might be fun after all."

Later, Shaggy Dog sat uncomfortably in the corner of the Grand Ballroom. His eyes took in the immense columns of marble, all three black stone fireplaces, and the vibrant artwork that hung around the room. He had just decided to slip away from all the sneers directed his way by the pompous court attendees when the Princess finally arrived. She was dressed not in layers of lace and ribbon but a simple – if not elegant – green dress. She had a thin smile as she entered to the cheers of all in attendance.

The Queen quickly called her daughter forward to stand before her. "Princess Sophia, let me be the first to say happy birthday this evening. You look quite lovely in that dress."

"Thank you, Momma.... Your Majesty. The dress is rather nice, and I can move so freely. Thank you for it," said the Princess quite sincerely.

"In the Kingdom of Crystal Forge, it is tradition for the Queen to hold an extravagant ball for the Princess's birthday," the Queen proclaimed for the entire room to hear.

The Princess felt the small glimmer of hope about this party slipping away. The rest of the court perked up in anticipation at the mention of a ball.

"However, my daughter is not traditional, and this is her day! So, without further ado..."

The Queen clapped her hands. Suddenly, servants rushed in from all directions. Some set up an archery range in one corner. Another group of servants set up a fishing-net throwing competition. Some started to roast apples in the fireplace while others set up a table laden with biscuits and honey. Other servants set up more fun and more unlikely games and food all around the ballroom.

The Princess thought it promised more fun than she had ever had within the castle walls.

And it was, too. She found it difficult to decide what was more enjoyable: climbing the rock wall or casting the nets or throwing knives. Maybe it was watching all the men and women of the court look so silly when trying to play any of these games. Regardless, she was having a great time. Even Shaggy Dog seemed to relax a bit, laughing at the courtiers in their discomfort. Evening turned to night, and the Princess was becoming more tired by the moment. She had just finished her third round with the throwing knives when she noticed a commotion at the center of the ballroom.

She made her way to where all the members of the court had gathered. In the midst of the semicircle stood a figure shrouded in a midnight black robe. He was tall and broad-shouldered, but the most striking aspect was the man did not possess a human head. Instead, his dark eyes wreathed with fire peered from a gigantic goat head. The Princess had no clue who he was, but Shaggy Dog recognized him almost immediately. The Princess saw Shaggy Dog's hair stand up and heard a low growl come from his chest.

Shaggy Dog had no love for the one called the Goat Head Sorcerer – none at all. He knew the mysterious sorcerer well, or at least well enough. He knew of the legions at his command. The Ravens of Despair answered to him. Their incessant cawing could drive a person to hopeless depression. The infamous Goblin Army that specialized in millions of tiny cuts to wear a person down were at his disposal. The Goat Head Sorcerer also had the likes of the Snake Oil Witches under his thumb. These vile creatures could place spells on a person and use fake potions or offer fake weapons which all led to false hope and distraction. The Goat Head Sorcerer had many more creatures and weapons to use for his evil purposes. The mere fact that he was here now was ominous.

The silence in the spacious ballroom felt tangible. No one dared move a muscle as the Goat Head Sorcerer raised his hateful eyes to the crowd. As his gaze swept across the room, so did trembling fear and anxiety. His eyes locked onto the Princess, and a wicked grin split his hairy face. In a whisper that, somehow, everyone could hear, he said, "I curse you."

Then he was simply gone. There was no puff of smoke, no bang, or flash of light. The fear and anxiety of the onlookers was now accompanied by shock, sadness, and guilty relief, the only evidence he had ever been there.

The first sound was the anguished cry of the Queen. There were no words, only a primal sound of fear, fury, and loss. Servants rushed quickly to her side to keep her from collapsing. Shaggy Dog sat near to the Princess, staring blankly at the spot the Goat Head Sorcerer had occupied moments ago. The Princess, still quite confused and becoming ever more so, just watched as the crowd broke into small groups, chattering quietly but urgently.

The Queen was the first to recover her senses and immediately ordered everyone but essential personnel out of the room. As the ballroom emptied, a guard attempted to usher the still shocked Shaggy Dog through the doorway. As if waking from a dream, Shaggy Dog bounded around the guard to remain at the Princess's side. The guard looked to the Queen, who waved him off with a resigned sigh. Standing beside her throne, she motioned for the pair to approach.

"My daughter, I am so sorry. If there was anything that could have prevented this curse on you, I would have seen it done." The Queen had become stoic, although her eyes were still full of tears.

The Princess was beginning to understand that this – whatever *this* was – was extremely serious.

"I'm afraid. I'm afraid because you all are afraid. I do not understand what is going on!" the Princess cried out as tears ran down her cheeks.

Shaggy Dog attempted to move closer to her, but he could not get much closer without knocking her down and lying on top of her.

The Queen moved down the steps and placed one arm across her shoulders. "It's quite alright to be afraid, my dear. We all are. You have been cursed by the most evil Goat Head Sorcerer. For what purpose, I cannot begin to understand. But I do know we can fight it. I have already sent for the Benevolent Witch to join us as soon as possible." The Queen looked into the beautiful, terrified face of her daughter. "She will know what steps to take to vanquish this evil."

The Queen, the Princess, and Shaggy Dog retired to the cozy confines of the study, where they found the Benevolent Witch awaiting them. Shaggy Dog thought the Benevolent Witch was difficult to describe. She appeared neither young nor old. She was not beautiful or plain. Her skin sometimes seemed milky white and other times appeared golden tan.

She offered a kind smile to the group, but there was no chit chat or small talk. Getting straight to the point, the Benevolent Witch asked about the encounter with the Goat Head Sorcerer. She seemed to think no detail was too small. After exhausting the scenario with accounts from everyone present, she focused on the Princess, asking how she had been feeling recently. She asked about her sight, her hearing and taste, and if she had experienced leg cramps or numbness in her fingers. The Benevolent Witch asked scores and scores of questions, and the Princess answered them all wearily. The Princess was beginning to wonder if the Benevolent Witch was really a Raven of Despair in disguise, given all her cawing. But finally, the Benevolent Witch stopped asking questions and stood in silence for a long time.

Shaggy Dog had started to become restless when the Benevolent Witch finally spoke. "Princess Sophia, dear, you have truly been cursed by the Goat Head Sorcerer himself. From what I have learned today, the curse is most vile and if you do not fight it – and *him* – it will surely be your demise. But do not dwell on what could be. Instead, focus your heart on the task that lies before you. For if you are strong and brave, and if you have just a spot of good luck, you will defeat the Goat Head Sorcerer and throw off this vile curse!"

The Princess, although still scared, saw hope in the Queen's eyes, as well as determination in the dark eyes of Shaggy Dog. She knew that with their help she could beat the ol' goat.

"What do I need to do?" she said.

The Benevolent Witch smiled. "You must go on a quest, like the bravest of knights. And you will have many adventures, though I will not promise they all will be pleasant. You will search for the Helm of Knowledge first. It is rumored to be with the witches of Houstonia. Then, with all courage you possess, you will continue on to find your weapon to use against the Goat Head Sorcerer. And, finally, there will be the inevitable battle. There is much I do not know about your quest, but the beginning and the search for the Helm is clear. I, of course, will check on you as often as I am able."

Then, much like the Goat Head Sorcerer, the Benevolent Witch was gone, but instead of leaving fear behind, she left tentative hope.

After only the briefest of moments, Shaggy Dog positioned himself in front of the Princess. He bowed his head low and made a formal request to accompany the Princess on her quest. The Princess was delighted and even the Queen smiled at Shaggy Dog's initiative. It seemed that a nervous excitement was replacing their earlier heavy fear that had fell over the room. The Queen motioned for a servant near the door, and he rolled a tall, shrouded rack into the center of the room.

"Princess, although I give you this gift with all of my heart, I never dreamed you would need it so soon or so dearly," the Queen stated. As the Princess pulled at the shroud, she continued, "This armor will help to protect you from many threats. It is light but durable. It is strong but flexible. The Armor of Love has magical properties as well. For example, it has the ability to mend itself, given time and care. I hope it aids you well on your quest."

The Princess's eyes were wide as she stared at the rose gold armor hanging before her. It was sleek and beautiful, but it was also a stark reminder of the seriousness of her situation. She accepted the gift from the Queen solemnly.

The next morning, the Princess and Shaggy Dog began traveling early. It was a long road to Houstonia though mostly easy riding. The Princess did not push her horse too hard; Shaggy Dog was trotting beside her, after all. She soon began to feel that same nervous excitement as she traveled farther from the castle than she had ever been without a full entourage. In the early morning light, they had passed through the farmland that surrounded the castle and entered the Queen's forest well before lunch. As they trotted through the small clearing that contained the giant, scarred oak, she realized that every inch forward would represent a new milestone. Every step would be one step farther from home than she had ever been. And so, the morning continued through a quick lunch and into the afternoon.

That night, Shaggy Dog found a smooth patch of ground next to tall rocks to act as shelter. There was no need for a fire on this warm night, and enough moonlight crept into their camp for them to see easily. For the most part, the Princess and Shaggy Dog sat in comfortable silence, listening to the sounds of the forest and consumed by their own thoughts. It was peaceful.

The next morning, after a quick, cold breakfast, they made another early start. By mid-morning, the duo emerged from the forest into dazzling sunlight. The forest continued on their left, and off to their right they thought they could see the mountains in the distance – or, at least, they knew they were there, so they *must* be seeing them. Before them were gently rolling hills with the occasional lone oak standing sentry. It was on the top of the fourth hill and under the second oak that they spotted the first tiny town on their journey. Shaggy Dog guessed they would reach the town just after lunch, and suggested they try to find a hot meal. The Princess eyed the tiny town and thought that a hot meal may be a long shot. It was not much of a town, really. But a shot at a hot meal was worth pushing a little harder.

When they had cut the distance to the town by half, they happened upon a woman in distress. She was frantically trying to right a cart still hitched to her mule. As excited as the woman was, surrounded by hundreds of packages and tiny bottles which were the former contents of her cart, the mule was quite the opposite. He was the color of weathered stone and might as well been made of it judging by his lack of movement. As the Princess and Shaggy Dog approached, the woman called out for help. Of course, the duo answered her call. In no time at all, the three of them had turned the cart upright. It took considerably more time to pick up the packages, bundles, and bottles littered all around, not to mention organizing everything. But eventually it was done, and all three sat down for a break.

"You are truly kind to help a lady you don't even know," said the woman. Shaggy Dog and the Princess took in the woman fully for the first time. She was quite striking, with her red hair and pale skin. A spray of freckles across her face did not distract from her beauty at all. In fact, they enhanced her green eyes and charming smile. She was wearing a hunter-green robe and her hair was pulled back in a single tie. She definitely appeared to be frazzled but only in a temporary way.

"It never occurred to me not to help," said the Princess. Shaggy Dog remained silent but alert. "I would assume you would do the same for anyone you happen across."

"Without a doubt, I will always lend a hand to anyone in need. I have made it my life's work, but you and I are in the minority, I am afraid. Most people would go out of their way to avoid helping out. It is the way of the world."

"That is so sad," the Princess lamented. Shaggy Dog looked at her as she continued, "But at least there are people like you that use their entire life to help others. How exactly do you do so?"

The woman swelled with pride and any trace of her disheveled state seemed to melt away. "I am a witch that has dedicated my life to fighting dark curses, using nature as my guide. I have studied from the Dragon Spine to Clear Lakeshire and everywhere in between. I help those who have lost hope, and I educate people before calamity strikes! I have found a cure for most curses that the snobby witches think are beneath them and therefore disregard." She sneered, but quickly her smile returned.

The Princess could hardly believe her luck – here was someone that could help her! Maybe she would not have to go on such a long quest after all. She could get a cure from this witch and be home within a couple of days.

"I think that is wonderful! I could so use your help, Madame Witch. I am actually on my way to Houstonia to seek the help of the witches there, but if you have a cure for evil curses, I won't have to go that far!" All of this came from the Princess in one breath. "I would be so grateful if you could help me."

"Well, it is fortunate I ran into you and your dog on this barren road. Tell me, girl, what type of curse afflicts you?"

The Princess told her all about the Goat Head Sorcerer and the night of her birthday. She told her about the words used so quietly by the vile one. She recounted the aftermath of whispers and fear. Then there was the meeting with the Benevolent Witch. Madame Witch seemed most interested in this conversation and asked many questions. Finally, the Princess told her of their quest, starting with the search for the Helm of Knowledge in Houstonia. She mentioned again how lucky she felt to have met Madame Witch so soon, and how excited she was to get a cure and go home. Madame Witch, for her part, gasped in all the right places. She was attentive and asked informed and probing questions. She had a gleam in her eyes that Shaggy Dog found to be off-putting. He couldn't quite put his nose on it, but something was not right about this witch.

Madame Witch rummaged through her cart and pulled out a large leather bag. She motioned for them to sit and opened the bag. She first pulled out letters explaining they were from people she had cured of one curse or another. The Princess was most impressed with the number of letters. Then Madame Witch pulled out a beautiful necklace and bragged that it was a gift from a wealthy merchant after one of her potions cured his wife. Again, the Princess was most impressed with the beautiful jewelry. Finally, Madame Witch pulled out a short, slender wooden rod. It was covered in writing the Princess did not recognize, and the glow at its tips could have only been gold. Madame Witch explained that this rod could determine exactly which of her miraculous cures would work for the Princess. She waved it over the Princess's head, muttering softly to herself.

"Most difficult... yes... yes. Oh, that is interesting... Most difficult..."

The Princess was on pins and needles until Madame Witch finally stopped waving her wand, closed her eyes, then mumbled as she placed the rod on her forehead. After a moment, her eyes flew wide open, and she shrieked. The Princess and Shaggy Dog both jumped back, startled by the outburst.

Madame Witch locked eyes with the Princess. "Young lady, you have a most serious curse. It will take quite a bit of my resources to cure it, but cure it I will. My magic rod has whispered your ailments to me, and I have divined a cure. It will take time and be very expensive to find all the ingredients needed to complete it. But we can get started right away."

With that, Madame Witch began digging in her cart again. She set up a small table and started unwrapping packages and pulling stoppers from bottles. She was mumbling to herself about how expensive this cure would be, but as a good witch she would help... yes... she would help.

Shaggy Dog stared at the witch as she mixed a potion for the Princess. He noticed she had added drops from the same bottle on three separate occasions. He thought she was just grabbing things at random to add as she muttered about how expensive it was going to be to create a cure. He nudged the Princess, and she bent down close to him. Shaggy Dog whispered, "Ask her what she wants in return for a cure. She does not know you are the Princess, and let's keep it that way."

"Madame Witch, I am forever grateful for your efforts. How can I ever repay you?"

"Oh, young one, I do this out of pleasure to help others. However, if you would like to donate to help me buy supplies... you know, I would be grateful. I would think a girl with armor such as yours would have coin to spare," the witch said with a hungry look.

"I do not have much money with me on this trip, but I could always pay you back," the Princess replied quietly.

Madame Witch stopped mixing the potion and turned to face the Princess. "These ingredients are not cheap! How do you expect me to provide a cure without any money to replenish my stores? Or to live on? How selfish are you that you would steal from a kindly witch?" Her demeanor had changed completely. She began repacking her supplies, then stopped and said, "I could take your armor as payment. You do have a quite serious curse on you, or at least that's what my spell told me."

The Princess looked down at her armor gleaming in the afternoon sun. She did not want to part with the armor the Queen had just given her, but for a cure, she would part with almost anything. She was about to agree when Shaggy Dog gave a low growl.

The witch looked at him nervously, exclaiming, "Control your beast, little one!"

"SNAKE OIL WITCH!" Shaggy Dog exclaimed angrily, baring his teeth. "That is all you are. You said a spell revealed her ailment but you only used your fancy rod and cast no spells! You are lying. You are a fraud and a cheat!"

The Princess was shocked, and was about to protest to defend the witch when she noticed her changing. The beautiful face was melting away to reveal an old hag underneath. The witch's sweet, charismatic voice was replaced with a raspy screech as she said, "I should have gotten rid of you, dog! I knew you were going to be trouble."

Shaggy Dog growled and backed away, beckoning with his head for the Princess to follow. The witch just glared as the duo started away.

"Shaggy Dog," the Princess said, "how did you know?"

"I had my suspicions early on, but I was hoping for a miracle cure. I should have been more level-headed, and she never would have gotten so far. I'm just glad you didn't drink the potion. Who knows what it could have caused?"

"Well, thank you, Shaggy Dog," said the Princess as they trotted down towards the town. "I didn't realize until now how badly I want to beat this curse and go home. Guess I am more scared than I realized."

"You do not have to thank me, Princess, and of course you are scared. We will just take it one step at time. And first of all, we could find something to eat – I'm starving."

"I knew it was serious when you growled. But when you spoke in front of a stranger, I really paid attention. Now all you can talk about is food!"

Shaggy Dog just wagged his tail and kept his rapid pace towards a hot meal.

The next few days were simple and almost happy. The duo traveled by day, taking short breaks to keep themselves from becoming tired out. They stopped early each evening to enjoy each other's company before going to sleep. They told stories and played games, and joked and laughed. Troubles and fears and curses seemed to be far away, or at least someone else's problem. The freedom of the open road, the beautiful scenery, and the excellent companionship made the trip to Houstonia pass quickly. It seemed that they had only just left the Snake Oil Witch when the sparkling gates came into view ahead.

Chapter 3

" Shoot! Be right back, guys," Brandee said over her shoulder as she rushed to make drinks for the impatient waitresses at the other end of the bar. I had not noticed how busy the college side of the bar had become.

Daniel had a far-off look in his eyes again, lost in his thoughts.

"Crystal Forge, is that right? Sounds like a crazy and amazing place," I said.

Daniel actually smiled – not ear to ear, but a real smile nonetheless. He pushed the empty bottle across the bar and said, "Truly wonderful."

"That goat head dude though, he sucks big time," I replied, draining the rest of my drink. Brandee rushed back over to us, out of breath.

"Yeah, he sucks. Bad dude, that one," was all Daniel said.

"Why did he curse her? The princess – why her in particular?" I asked.

"I don't know if anyone knows why he did what he did. Some people's lifestyle made it easy for him to curse them. But for her? The curse was just an act of random evil," Daniel said through a rigid jaw as his hands clenched into tight fists.

"I think the Princess was very brave," offered Brandee.

Daniel's hands flattened upon the bar, and he cocked his head slightly. "How so?"

"She barely hesitated. She was scared, but she didn't let it engulf her, paralyze her. Without a second thought, she set off to beat the curse," said Brandee.

Daniel laughed a little.

"Sure did. She didn't complain or fret. She just wanted to beat him. She was so strong."

Brandee brought over another round, even though Daniel shook his head. The older woman who had been sitting with her husband at the end of the bar returned from the restroom and sat one seat closer to Daniel. He did not seem to notice.

"I thought Shaggy was gonna rip that witch apart right at the end," I said.

Daniel's knuckles turned white on the hand that held the bottle. He took a big swig of his beer before saying, "Shaggy Dog was pissed. He was mad at everything, and just the fact someone tried to take advantage of the situation set him off. I don't know how he didn't rip the witch apart. Probably didn't want the Princess to see him do it."

I drew away as Daniel leaned toward me with bulging eyes. Brandee acted quickly, years of breaking up bar fights giving her a sixth sense, and said, "Well, what happened next? Or was that it?"

Tense moments passed until Daniel started talking again. Each word he spoke had a small piece of his pent-up anger attached. Eventually, his shoulders relaxed and his voice calmed.

"Not the end, but it was the end of the beginning, I guess," he said. "The duo arrived at Houstonia and then travelled farther. They met many friends. And the real fight against the curse got started. No, that wasn't the end, not yet."

Chapter 4

Houstonia, home to the Witches of Truth, was a true marvel. It was a vast and sprawling place. It could not be described as a castle or a palace because it was simply too big. It could not be described as a city because it was simply too grand. The wall that housed the gates was twenty feet high and bright white. The gates themselves were shiny gold and were almost as tall as the wall. Eight horses could easily walk side by side through the gateway with room to spare. Within the walls, the outer courtyard held a five-level fountain. It was solid black marble, and the water streaming down it changed colors from yellow to red to blue to green. Past the fountain was the inner gate. Although not as tall as its outer counterpart, it was no less splendid. Along each rail of the golden gate were intricate designs. Countless hours had been spent hand-carving each shape and line. Beyond the inner gate, the true wonder of Houstonia was on display. Buildings almost as large as Seascape Castle stood in every direction. The building directly before the gate had more glass windows on the front than most cities had in total. It was here that the duo began their search for the Helm of Knowledge.

As they approached the glass-fronted building, they were met by a handsome witch called Reserio. He informed them that the Benevolent Witch had sent word ahead, so their arrival was expected. During their stay in Houstonia, Reserio was to be a tour guide of sorts. He was tall, with a charming smile and an inviting demeanor. He did not seem at all put off by Shaggy Dog's disheveled appearance, or the fact the Princess had not had a bath in a few days. He seemed only eager to help get them acclimated to all that Houstonia had to offer.

After the Princess had washed up and Shaggy Dog had obstinately *not* washed up, Reserio started to reveal to them the wonders of Houstonia. He showed them a building filled with witches researching and battling minor curses such as lesions on the skin. The next building, also full of witches, was for researching and battling more severe curses, such as curses of the head or bones. Reserio then took them to yet another grand building where the witches were working on preventive spells and potions. Shaggy Dog had no idea there were so many witches dedicated to doing battle with the Goat Head Sorcerer and his minions. It gave him a sense of hope to know that all these smart, powerful witches were working tirelessly for the greater good.

The Princess just felt exhausted. It was only early in the afternoon, but she knew she had to take a rest or she may pass out in the next building. Reserio suggested resting in the shade of an old elm tree which stood on the banks of a swift river directly in front of the next building they were to tour.

As the Princess leaned back against the tree, Shaggy Dog studied the white granite building and tried to guess the wonders housed within its walls.

Reserio asked softly, "Do you see that line of little furry creatures crossing the river on that log?"

"I do not see any creatures," replied the Princess dreamily.

But Shaggy Dog did. They were only about the size of small squirrels, but definitely not shaped long and fast like squirrels. Instead, these creatures resembled oversized, fuzzy peaches with legs, arms, and ears. They waddled out onto the log in a long, straight line that seemed endless. Shaggy Dog could see a hundred, if not more, and the line was moving steadily.

"Just up the river a bit, Princess. Yes, right there. Those are known as the Plumplins, and they are curious creatures to say the least," Reserio said in a tender tone. "Each day, every Plumplin that is able crosses the river to scour for food, eat its fill, and bring back some for those too young or too old to do so. One of the first lessons we witches learn when arriving at Houstonia involves the Plumplins. You see, when one of them falls into the river, that is like being cursed by the Goat Headed Sorcerer. Now, most Plumplins never fall into the river once during their whole lives, but some do. Some of those fall into the still water near the edge, where it is relatively easy for them to climb out again and resume their lives. For some reason, not all that fall into the still water climb back out, and the still water eventually drowns them. Some fall near to that branch, in the slightly swifter-moving water. It is still relatively easy for these Plumplins to reach the safety of the shore, but sometimes their bodies are slammed into the branch on the way down or are pulled beneath the surface by the current. Those Plumplins may still survive but will be permanently injured. Finally, some of them fall into the swiftest-moving part of the river. If we do not throw them a lifeline quickly, they never make it out again. Ultimately, what would be best for the Plumplins is to be shielded from ever falling into the river to begin with," Reserio said, ending his speech quietly.

The Princess was not positive she grasped Reserio's intended message and could not think of an appropriate response. So, she remained silent. She just watched the Plumplins as they marched across the log one after another in a seemingly endless procession. As she watched them, she wondered which part of the river she had fallen into.

The next few days were filled with constant motion interrupted by frequent and progressively longer breaks. Shaggy Dog was beginning to grow concerned about the Princess's lack of stamina as they traveled through the buildings learning as much as they could. The Princess, for her part, never complained. She walked as much as she could and only took breaks when absolutely necessary. Even those breaks frustrated her. She felt she should be doing more and doing it faster to earn her Helm. Reserio was with them every step of the way and assured them many times that they were on the correct path. He spun everything in a positive manner. If the Princess was frustrated in taking a break, Reserio would use the time to discuss potion application or spell theory. If Shaggy Dog was worrying himself sick, Reserio would point out that the Princess was working really hard to gain her Helm, so of course she was getting tired. Learning and walking. Asking and answering questions. Breaks and more breaks. That was their life during the days in Houstonia, until one morning Reserio met them outside the small cottage the duo had been sharing. Upon his face was a larger than normal grin.

The Helm of Knowledge was ready if the Princess thought she was up to the task. Though the Princess and Shaggy Dog had no idea what the task might be, she gave affirmation after only a brief hesitation.

Reserio led them to a part of Houstonia where they had spent very little time. He called it the 'factory corner'. The buildings here were smaller and more practical. Most were constructed from plain stone and were no higher than three stories. Just like the rest of Houstonia, the factory corner was clean and extremely well maintained. Reserio directed them to a round building in the center of the area, positioned like the hub of a wheel with streets radiating from it. Reserio explained that the building was indeed called the Hub. All the finishing work and fine refinement of all the projects from other buildings was completed here, and it was here the Princess would finally discover whether she had what it took to gain the Helm of Knowledge.

They were still lost in the grandeur of the circular room when Reserio spoke. "Quite a sight to see, isn't it? And yet, despite all of our knowledge and considerable skill, there are curses the Goat Head Sorcerer uses that still confound us."

He gestured to a hallway to the right and led the way. The simple stone hallway shortly led to a staircase.

They went up the wooden steps, Reserio leading, followed by the Princess with Shaggy Dog bringing up the rear. Shaggy Dog was close on her heels, and even Reserio had a little extra in his step as he bounded up the staircase. It seemed she was the only one with a knot of dread growing in her stomach. She could not quite figure out exactly what was causing this fear. Shaggy Dog was right to be excited about all the amazing weapons and armor the witches of Houstonia had produced. And, surely, Reserio's excitement meant he was positive she would gain her Helm of Knowledge today, so she could not come up with one plausible reason why she felt she should turn around and escape down the stairs. Every step she took up the staircase, the knot in her stomach grew a little more.

Then they were at the top of the stairs facing a lone door, and the time to escape had slipped away. There was only one way forward, and it was through the door. She steeled herself and found the dread in her stomach diminished.

They passed through the doorway into a cozy room with a small crackling fire. Four plush, velvety chairs encircled a small wooden table in the center of the room. The walls were mostly bare except for one painting on the left-hand side, which depicted a boy younger than the Princess. He appeared tired and sore. His clothes were soiled and torn. The scabbard on his belt was empty. The boy appeared to be struggling to climb a steep hill to reach the summit. Waiting at the top, suspended in a pillar of light, was a pair of angel wings. It was a beautifully accomplished piece of art that made the Princess both sad and hopeful for the boy.

Sitting in one of the chairs was a witch that resembled an older, rougher Reserio. He did not smile, nor did he rise from his seat as the group entered. Only when the Princess noticed him did he stand and greet them all.

"Welcome, Princess, to the Room of Choice. My name is Anderserio. And I will be the final witch you must speak with on this visit to Houstonia," he said in a deep, resonating tone.

Reserio rolled his eyes and scoffed, "Drop the theatrics, Anderserio. That is my department!"

"My good brother, whatever do you mean?"

"The Room of Choice? Ha! It's just the sitting room for your workshop, you sot!"

Then Reserio stepped forward and hugged him. Anderserio reciprocated with a hearty laugh.

"Wait, so you two are really brothers?" inquired the Princess.

"Unfortunately, it is so," said Reserio with a smile.

Anderserio chuckled as they all settled into chairs. "Princess, I did not realize your companion walked on four legs or I would have had a more suitable seating arrangement for him."

Shaggy Dog simply leapt onto the unoccupied chair and stared intently at Anderserio with a mocking glare.

"Never mind, then!"

From that point on, there was little in the form of pleasantries, as Anderserio immediately addressed the issue at hand. He explained that the Helm of Knowledge the Princess was to receive was not *the* Helm but simply *a* Helm. There were many, and each was made specifically for the wearer. The Helm was constructed in Houstonia and the final touches were completed by him. Many witches from all different buildings had placed spells upon it, imparted knowledge, and added power to the Helm during the process. Now that it was complete, the Helm of Knowledge would provide the Princess with the instincts needed to battle the curse and the Goat Head Sorcerer himself. While wearing the Helm, she would know which potion to take for the greatest benefit, or which weapon would cause her enemy the most damage. It would not speak to her, but if she listened and trusted her instincts, the answers would be clear.

Then, with a small flourish of Anderserio's hands, the Helm of Knowledge appeared in the middle of the small table. It was quite beautiful. It was the same light rose gold as the Princess's armor, and was smooth all around with ample protection for her head and back of the neck. The face was left open except where it wrapped slightly across the cheek area. The Princess sensed the power humming from the Helm, and she could not keep her eyes off of it.

"Do you accept these terms, Princess?" asked Anderserio quietly.

"I'm sorry, sir. I was lost in thought and mesmerized by its beauty. I did not hear the terms."

"You may take the Helm of Knowledge and use it for as long as your battle takes. Then it must be returned here. All you have to do is pledge to fight with all your being and to help any others you can in their own struggle. Do you accept these terms that have been laid out for you?" asked Anderserio again, a little more forcefully.

"Of course. I will be honored to wear such a fine piece of armor," the Princess answered. She pulled her gaze away from the Helm to look at Shaggy Dog. He too, was staring intently at the Helm in anticipation, eager to put it to the test and defeat the curse as soon as possible.

"Then the Helm is yours, my Princess," stated Reserio. His brother beamed. "Use it well."

"I don't understand," said Shaggy Dog. "I thought there was a task to complete or test to pass?"

The Princess nodded in agreement. Reserio chuckled quietly then said, "Yes. Sorry about misleading you. We Witches of Truth seek out truth but don't always speak plainly. It has been discovered through the trials of others before you who came seeking help against a curse that focusing on a future task allows us to do our work easier. In each building, you answered questions from witches and passed through revealing spells to help us gain the knowledge needed for the Helm."

"I see," said the Princess. "You could have just told me."

"Perhaps, but experience has taught us different," replied Reserio. "All we want is for you to defeat this curse. The Helm is the best we can do to help you on your quest."

The next morning, Shaggy Dog and the Princess were set to depart. They had accomplished their first major goal on the quest. Although they were not exactly sure what was next, they knew it would not lie within the walls of Houstonia. They had spent much of the night discussing where to go next. Shaggy Dog had felt that a visit to the salt flats would be good, to help restore some of the Princess's strength that the curse was draining away. The Princess had tried to convince Shaggy Dog that there was a good reason to travel to the Dragon Spine – though in truth her only reason was that she had always wanted to see the mountains. The rest of the night had been filled with Shaggy Dog sleeping and the Princess wearing the Helm and trying to get it to tell her something, until she too fell asleep.

Reserio was again waiting for them outside their building, and he invited them to breakfast, saying that there were several guests they may like to see before they departed.

The dining hall was on the way to the stables and the gate, so the duo brought their travel packs with them, eager to be on the road once more. Shaggy Dog looked a little odd carrying both his and the Princess's packs on his back, but he did not mind. The Princess held her Helm under her arm and was fully outfitted in the Armor of Love. She liked the light clinking noises as she walked, a reassuring sound like little bells, which constantly reminded her of her mother and home. She hoped they could eat a quick breakfast, say their goodbyes, and be on the road soon. She wanted to put the Helm to the test.

As they entered the dining hall, they both noticed there were more people than normal at this hour. All chatter silenced and every eye turned towards them. The silence lingered and seemed to grow. Then, from somewhere at the back, came a cry of, "We believe in you Princess!" followed immediately by an uproar that could have been heard clear across the Forge. The Princess saw the Queen standing amongst the crowd cheering along with everyone else. She noticed through her blurry vision that the Queen had tears in her eyes as well. Even Shaggy Dog looked taken aback: he sat on his haunches with the packs on his back, looking blankly at the crowd with wide eyes. It was a glorious reception.

The Benevolent Witch approached them. Speaking briefly, she told them not to leave without speaking privately with her first. Next were several of the servants from the castle. They wished the Princess well and all agreed she had grown at least an inch since she had been on the road. Everyone was smiling and happy as they congratulated her on acquiring the Helm of Knowledge. Everyone seemed to believe that she was going to beat back the Goat Head Sorcerer and end his curse upon her.

Finally, as the crowd simmered down, the Queen approached. Everyone backed away to create a pocket of space. Even Shaggy Dog edged back. The Princess started to curtsy, but the Queen stopped her with a warm embrace. The tears were no longer contained within her eyes, instead they spilled down the Queen's cheeks as she hugged the Princess tightly. Finally, after what could have been moments or hours, they separated.

"My daughter, I am so proud you have started to meet this threat head on," spoke the Queen gently.

"I never had any intention to do otherwise," replied the Princess in confusion.

"I know, but I was worried that after traveling here and seeing all this: the grandeur, all the witches working tirelessly..." she gestured with both arms out wide, "that maybe... Oh, never mind! I am just so proud of you. Now, let me see your Helm."

The Princess showed the Queen her new Helm. She explained to her the details that Anderserio had revealed. Then, she told the Queen all about her experience in

Houstonia and the Plumplins. She bragged about Reserio and the splendor of the buildings. The Queen nodded, gasped, laughed, and asked all the right questions.

Before either of them knew it, the morning had almost entirely passed. Shaggy Dog approached and mentioned in a low voice that perhaps the Princess might like to eat some breakfast before it was actually lunch that she would be eating. All three of them laughed. It was not until the Princess was detailing their encounter with the Snake Oil Witch that any tension filled the room. The Queen immediately wanted to send her off with a battalion of her finest soldiers. No daughter of hers would be bothered by the likes of that Snake Oil Witch in her own kingdom. But the Princess reminded her that this was *her* quest, and besides, that many men in full armor and with wagons for stores would only slow them down.

When it was past time to leave and the duo had said all their goodbyes, Reserio approached the Princess. He gave her several items for her quest, from different witches from Houstonia. These included a dozen or so small potions, and he explained the varied properties of each in turn. There were several packages of blue powder to help ease any stomach-related issues. He also gifted her a supple leather belt with pouches and pockets to hold all these items. He said Anderserio had spent most of the night making it, but that he was too stubborn to present it himself.

Just when the Princess thought he was finished, Reserio reached behind him and brought out a sword.

"This you may have seen on the wall earlier in your visit," he said solemnly.

The Princess did not know if she had seen this exact sword, but it was beautiful. It was small and double edged. The blade was a shiny silver color, and the handle was a rough dark wood.

"I do not recall, but it is quite the weapon."

"I do not believe this to be your *true* weapon, or perhaps it is. Regardless, I feel this sword will serve you well. Its name is Aggressio. It was my father's blade. My brother and I would be honored if you carried it with you on your quest," Reserio said as he passed her the sword and scabbard.

"The honor is all mine," replied the Princess, bowing her head first to Reserio and then to Anderserio, who stood in the corner. Shaggy Dog nudged her impatiently, and again they made a round to say farewells before heading to the stable.

The duo did not spend much time at the stable. The Princess's horse had been fed and saddled by the stable hand and was eager to leave its stall far behind. Once the Princess had transferred the bags from Shaggy Dog's back to their new packhorse that the Queen had insisted upon, they were on the move. They walked quickly through Houstonia, through the beautiful inner gate, across the courtyard with the colorful fountain, and beyond the impressive outer gate.

At the first crossroads they reached, Shaggy Dog looked at the Princess with a questioning glance.

"I'm not real sure which way to go now," she said. Houstonia lay behind them, and the whole world was before them.

"Perhaps you should have spent a few moments with me like I had asked you to," said a voice from behind them.

Shaggy Dog whirled around; teeth bared to defend against a surprise attack.

"I could have set you on the correct track hours ago instead of chasing you for the better part of the afternoon," said the Benevolent Witch.

The Princess had the courtesy to look embarrassed as she said, "I am so sorry. With the excitement of my mother's arrival, Reserio gifting me this amazing sword, and all the people wishing me luck, as well as Shaggy Dog pushing me to the door, and—"

"It's fine, my sweet child," interrupted the Benevolent Witch. "I apologize for sounding so harsh a moment ago. I am here with you now. That is all that matters, after all. Come, let's sit. We have much to discuss, and I know you are both anxious to get on the road to defeating the curse."

The three sat in the short grass under two wide oaks. The sun had crested hours before, but the heat of the day was still on them. The Benevolent Witch wasted little time: she congratulated the Princess on coming this far but cautioned that this was only the beginning. She said that the duo should continue their quest to the east, and must travel to the Dragon Spine Mountains, where there was a canyon that could only be found by those seeking it. Inside, the Princess would find her true weapon, by which she could battle the Goat Head Sorcerer.

"When we get into the canyon – what did you call it? The Canyon of Future Yesterdays? When we get there, will her weapon just be lying on the canyon floor?" asked an irritated Shaggy Dog.

"Why, noble canine, I have not the slightest idea what you two will discover, or how you will uncover it.

I just know she must seek her weapon there," replied the Benevolent Witch haughtily.

Shaggy Dog began a retort, but the Princess quickly said, "Then that is where we shall go. To the Canyon of Future Yesterdays."

The Benevolent Witch seemed mollified, and departed from under the trees quickly. Shaggy Dog watched as she disappeared more quickly than would be considered natural even by his standards.

"The Canyon of Future Yesterdays... Stupid-name Canyon, more like it," growled Shaggy Dog.

"It is a rather peculiar name."

"And she called me a canine! I should have... Well, she shouldn't have called me that."

"She isn't wrong. And you must forgive her, Shaggy Dog – she is under a great deal of strain."

"I don't have to forgive her anything," replied Shaggy Dog. "But at least she gave us a destination."

"And it is so far away. I guess we should get going," replied the Princess as she mounted her horse. She turned her steed east and started off at a trot. They had a long way to travel, a very long way indeed.

Chapter 5

Shaggy Dog slowed from a trot to a walk, then stopped completely. His ears perked up and the hair on his back raised as he looked ahead at a densely wooded hill. The Princess stopped her mount next to him. Shaggy Dog had become rigid as his eyes locked on the distant hill, never blinking.

After several moments, the Princess asked what he was staring at, but Shaggy Dog did not answer. His attention never wavered. He remained perfectly still.

Seconds turned into minutes. Just as the Princess about to ask him what he was looking at again, she heard it. The crash sounded as if a full-size tree had been snapped in two, then been hurled away. Shaggy Dog's ears had flattened, and a growl escaped his throat.

"What in the realm could that be?" asked the Princess, she too now staring at the dense woods.

"Nothing good. Let's veer away from there. We can cross the river farther south at Howling Head, or even Biscayne if we have to," said Shaggy Dog, still not moving his focus from the wooded hill.

"But that will add days to the journey!"

"Better to add days than have to face whatever that is, Princess," Shaggy Dog replied.

As they started to move off the road and cross the field away from the noise, the Princess spotted an eagle circling high over the wooded hill.

"That has to be the biggest eagle ever! Look at it, Shaggy Dog," she said, pointing to the sky.

Shaggy Dog tilted his head to look up. "Now what would a noble one be doing mixed up in whatever is going on over there?"

"Maybe we should go and find out," offered the Princess hopefully.

Before he could respond, another booming crash came from the hill.

"Where did the eagle go?" asked the Princess.

"It's almost directly above us. This is getting stranger by the moment," answered Shaggy Dog.

The duo watched as the eagle circled them, then dipped close to the ground only to rise up and circle them again. Each time the eagle dropped, it angled itself towards the wooded hill before rising again and circling.

"I think it wants us to follow it," said the Princess.

"It would seem that way. I'm not sure that would be such a good idea, Princess."

"She seems pretty adamant. Let's go and have a look," said the Princess, already moving in the direction that the eagle was indicating.

Shaggy Dog grumbled but followed along. The eagle still circled high above and still occasionally dipped down just ahead of them, urging them forward.

The wooded hill had not seemed so far away, but it took them over an hour to reach the edge of the forest. The trees were old, and their large trunks supported a massive, interlocked canopy. The absence of underbrush in the dim light under the trees was startling. Now unable to see the eagle, the Princess had second thoughts about this little adventure.

Before she could mention her thoughts of regret to Shaggy Dog, a loud crash shook them both. The trees in front of them were swaying, and the ground beneath their feet was shaking. A massive, oblong boulder came crashing through the trees right towards them.

The Princess's horse bucked wildly to the left, tossing her to the ground directly in the boulder's path. The wide-eyed Princess was rooted in place.

Shaggy Dog leapt to her side, nudging and pushing frantically trying to get the Princess to move. He barked his desire for her to move out of the way of the boulder.

Then the boulder that was barreling towards the Princess came to an abrupt stop.

The boulder made a most un-boulder-like moan.

The Princess's hand came away from her head without a trace of blood. At least she had not struck her head hard... but she was sure she had heard the boulder moan. She glanced at Shaggy Dog, and he shrugged his big shoulders as only a dog is able to do.

The boulder moaned again and began to sit up. It was not a rock at all, but a giant.

The Princess stared as Shaggy Dog renewed his efforts to get her to move. She could not stop staring at the big ears and big nose under the curly brown hair on the humongous head of the giant. She estimated the hulking figure was at least ten feet tall when standing. She was surprised he didn't have a beard. All the giants in stories had long, rough beards.

Shaggy Dog stopped nudging her and instead pulled her by the boot, straining to get her to safety. The giant moaned again and a large tear ran down his smooth cheek.

"Something must be wrong with him," said the Princess.

"That should make it easier for us to get away, then," snarled Shaggy Dog, never releasing her foot as he continued to try to drag her away from the giant. The giant, noticing them for the first time, quickly scooted away striking the trunk of an ancient tree. He cried out in pain this time and more tears flowed. Shaggy Dog, realizing there was no immediate threat, released the Princess's foot and moved to stand guard between her and the giant. The giant's eyes locked on Shaggy Dog, and he became still as stone.

A rustling of leaves behind the duo caused them to whirl around quickly. Perched on a log not fifteen feet away was the eagle that had directed them here. As they watched, the eagle started to grow taller and change. Before even a startled exclamation could escape the Princess's throat, an elf stood on the log in place of the eagle. She was tall and slender, and her dark hair matched her dark skin and eyes. She had two eagle feathers in her hair above her left ear. Her clothing was a natural-colored flexible material that stopped short of her knees and elbows.

She hopped down smoothly from the log, saying, "I have been trying to help this brute for two days. Every time I get close, he starts wailing and thrashing. Then he's off again. I'm not even sure what ails him."

An elf and a giant! The Princess's mouth hung open as the elf approached, stepping lightly without snapping a single twig or rustling a single leaf. Only the movement of the giant brought the Princess out of rapt amazement. The giant had leaned forward and was staring at Shaggy Dog intently.

With the elf only feet away, the Princess encouraged Shaggy Dog to move a little closer to the giant, whose eyes never left Shaggy Dog. Shaggy Dog was halfway between them and the giant when the giant smiled through his tears.

The Princess giggled quietly. "He is a funny-looking dog, but he is a good boy."

The giant's head jerked up in surprise, and he started sobbing again. Shaggy Dog looked at the Princess, then took a couple steps closer to the giant and sat down.

"Have you ever seen a dog before?" asked the Princess gently.

The giant shook his head.

"He has soft, thick fur. It would look nicer if he'd let me brush it every now and then."

The giant's breathing slowed, but his gaze was still focused intently on Shaggy Dog.

"Amazing," muttered the elf.

"I like to pet his coat," said the Princess as she approached Shaggy Dog. "Sometimes I'll pet him until he falls asleep." She reached out slowly to pat Shaggy Dog's head gently. "Do you want to pet him?"

The giant shook his head shyly and said, "Aargh dough."

Shaggy Dog took a few more cautious steps forward. Tentatively, the giant reached out a burly hand and brushed Shaggy Dog's back. Then his face split wide open in the biggest smile the Princess had ever seen. The tears were gone. The elf, the Princess, and the giant were all smiling and laughing. Even Shaggy Dog seemed to relax a bit, his tail swishing slowly back and forth.

Later that evening, after the elf had found a suitable campsite and started a small fire, she left them lounging peacefully to scout the area. She brought back berries and fresh water. They ate quietly, scared to break the peace with their coarse voices.

Finally, the elf said, "I hail from the east of the Dragon Spine Mountains, in the Heart of Viana. My name is too long for most non-elves to pronounce, but you may call me Sasha."

"My name is Sophia, and that is Shaggy Dog. We are both from the coast," replied the Princess.

"I know who you are, Princess. You bear a striking resemblance to your grandfather – not in looks, but in bearing. I knew him and liked him well." The comfortable silence draped back over the group. The Princess busied herself interweaving long blades of grass, and Sasha watched as the giant stroked a slumbering Shaggy Dog.

"That is an interesting dog you have, Sophia," noted Sasha after some time.

The Princess laughed out loud. "He's not my dog, that's for sure. I belong to him way more than he belongs to me. If he was awake, he'd probably say something about nobody belonging to anybody without mutual adoration, or some other nonsense," said the Princess.

"He can talk?" asked Sasha.

"He can. He just holds his tongue around those he doesn't know well."

"He seems to be a loyal companion. Still, it makes me wonder why a talking dog is traveling the countryside with the only heir to Seascape, all alone," probed Sasha.

The Princess looked down at the grass in her hands for a long time before responding. "I was cursed by the Goat Head Sorcerer, and we are on a quest in which speed and stealth are needed." She recounted the quest to Sasha, sparing no details. Once she started talking, it all spilled out. Sasha sat perfectly still and listened intently without interruption. As the Princess's tale approached their current circumstances, the giant shifted.

"Argh Dane!!!" he exclaimed.

The Princess and Sasha exchanged worried glances.

"That's his name. Dane. He says his name is Dane," said a sleepy Shaggy Dog, before putting his head back down and immediately falling asleep again.

Morning came quick and bright. The Princess rose to the rumbling snores of Dane, or at least so she thought. As it turned out, it was Shaggy Dog that had shaken the leaves on the trees with his snores all night. Sasha had left a breakfast for the group but was nowhere to be found. The Princess checked on the horses and busied herself doing small jobs around camp until everyone else stirred. It did not take long for Sasha to return with an armful of leafy plants. Without saying a word, she started boiling the plants over the small campfire. Shaggy Dog rose from his slumber next, and growled about a decent breakfast before setting to it. Sasha probed Shaggy Dog with questions about Dane, as the giant himself still slept peacefully under the trees. Shaggy Dog revealed that Dane had been running for a while, but Shaggy Dog was unsure what had caused him to flee. Shaggy Dog was able to discover the main reason for the giant's thrashing and bashing yesterday was an injury to his foot. Sasha nodded at each of Shaggy Dog's short answers and smiled when he mentioned the foot injury.

"Why do you smile, elf?" asked Shaggy Dog harshly.

"Not because I want to see the giant in pain – I can assure you of that, my four-legged friend," stated Sasha. "I smiled because I noticed his injury last night after he calmed down. I was up before the sun to find leaves of a julerpin palm to treat it. They are boiling over the fire as we speak."

"Hmmph," was the only reply Shaggy Dog could muster.

"He did not give you any indication what he was running from?" asked the Princess.

"No and I didn't press it," Shaggy Dog stated firmly.

"No matter. I will tend to his wound, and you two can be on your way by lunch," said Sasha.

"Fine by me," replied Shaggy Dog, gazing over at the slumbering Dane.

Hours later, when Dane finally stirred, Sasha was able to treat the small wound on his foot with the help of Shaggy Dog keeping Dane still. The Princess understood the giant much more readily this morning, though he spoke less often than Shaggy Dog. Dane's tribe called the hostile northern facing cliffs of the Dragon Spine Mountains home. It was a small tribe but widely known for its ferocity. None were more ferocious than Dane's father, the tribal chieftain. Over two weeks ago, the tribe was offered a position of power from the Goat Head Sorcerer in exchange for certain unnamed favors. The tribal elders were on the ridge about which way to go, but Dane was sure they were going to accept the offer. He saw no benefit in helping the Goat Head Sorcerer, who had never helped them before. So, he spoke out against the Goat Head Sorcerer and the offer. He was forced to flee in fear of retaliation from the Goat Head Sorcerer or his minions. He was lost, tired, and hungry. When he hurt his foot two days ago, he lost control. He felt better now, though, he told them.

The giant's tale lasted well into the afternoon. It was not a particularly long story full of detail, but Dane did not get in any hurry to tell it. Combined with the need to repeat himself endlessly to be understood and charades for words he did not know, most of the day was gone by the end of the telling. He was so tired by the end that he took a late afternoon nap in the warm sun. He was not the only one: Shaggy Dog was right next to him snoring just as fiercely. The Princess found herself alone at the campfire watching Sasha cook a meager supper.

"Do you two plan on leaving in the morning?" asked Sasha.

"Shaggy Dog normally does the planning," replied the Princess, glancing at the slumbering dog. "He'll want to push on."

"Probably wise to push forward and seek the canyon," said Sasha, "but you could stay for a few days and rest. I could teach you how to be more efficient in gathering supplies from the wilderness and maybe how to shoot a bow."

"That sounds great, but Shaggy Dog will want to be on the move," replied the Princess.

"He will, but I will talk to him," continued Sasha. "I think the only way Dane will let me help him further is if Shaggy Dog is close by."

"What are you going to do for the giant?"

"That is up to Dane. I know the people on the other side of the great grass sea, and they would take him in. Or Dane may want to go back to his tribe. He will need help, either way."

"That is so selfless and brave," said the Princess.

Sasha's eyebrows rose and she tilted her head. "Brave? Why do you say that?"

"Well, you're going to do something that could get you hurt, and you know it. But you're going to do it anyway," said the Princess quietly. "I think that is brave."

Sasha laughed. "Well, thank you, Princess. That is why life is so difficult to understand at times."

It was the Princess's turn to be confused. "What do you mean?"

"You said it is brave of me to do something that I know might get me hurt, right?" Sasha asked.

The Princess nodded.

"Some would say it is foolish to do something you know is going to hurt. Foolishness and bravery are very closely linked. That, my Princess, is why life is so difficult to understand."

Silently, the sun started its descent from the world for the night. The evening birds were singing their sweet, sad farewells to the daylight. The crickets and frogs were loud as a gentle breeze swept over the Princess. She stared towards the mountains to the east, thinking, *Yes. Life is difficult to understand.*

Four days later, the duo left Sasha and Dane early in the morning. Shaggy Dog was eager to move forward with the search for the canyon and a way to defeat the Goat Head Sorcerer. The Princess, on the other hand, had allowed the pleasant days with new friends to lull her into complacency. Sasha had taught her and Shaggy Dog how to better scavenge for necessary supplies in the wild. The Princess had learned how to draw and shoot a bow. Dane had gifted Shaggy Dog his bracelet, which Shaggy Dog now wore like a collar, and to the Princess he gave a chunk of shiny rock that, according to him, "Tastes funny." She had so enjoyed their time together, and now felt anxious and nervous as they set off on an easterly course. The road was well worn but smooth, and traveling was easy. Shaggy Dog had little difficulty keeping pace with the Princess on her mount. The rhythm of riding and the beautiful weather helped ease the Princess's doubt and worry. With the wind in her face and sun on her back, it was easy to know that they were on the correct path, and that they would soon find the canyon.

The plan was simple: wake up early, eat breakfast, travel east till dusk, and then set up camp only to do it all over again the next day. On the second day, shortly after breaking camp, Shaggy Dog pointed out a large herd of deer to the north. Later that same day, they quite literally stumbled upon a talking jackrabbit. After many apologies and promises to be more careful, the duo kept pushing east. The next morning, Shaggy Dog became impatient with the Princess. A baby possum had become separated from his family, and the Princess would not take another step till they were reunited. Mama possum seemed grateful... at least, she didn't hiss at them much. After the delay, Shaggy Dog cut their breaks short and pushed the horses hard to make up for lost time.

Shortly after dusk, it happened for the first time. The minions of the Goat Head Sorcerer attacked.

The Princess was tired and asked Shaggy Dog if they could make camp. The day had been hot, and they had traveled many miles after helping the baby possum. Shaggy Dog led them off the road to a patch of trees and what sounded like a small stream coming from a group of rocks to the north. The Princess was eager to shed her heavy armor and relax by a small fire and drinking fresh spring water. As she laid the Helm of Knowledge on the ground she felt, rather than saw, Shaggy Dog tense. Then she heard a twig snap in the patch of trees, and then Shaggy Dog gave a guttural growl. When she looked up, she saw a multitude of goblins streaming towards them. They were half her size, but they were armored with boiled leather and armed with thin, sharp swords. As they got closer, the goblins' battle shrieks threatened to drown out Shaggy Dog's menacing growl. She barely had time to unsheathe her sword, Aggressio, before the goblins were on top of them.

The goblins attacked in unorganized chaos. Several times, the Princess heard goblin squeals of pain that were not caused by her sword or Shaggy Dog's teeth. Her armor absorbed most of the strikes that made it past her sword and Shaggy Dog, who was snarling ferociously, repelling goblin after goblin. The numbers of their attackers never seemed to diminish even as the Princess slashed and stabbed, finding her mark time after time. The goblins had scored small cuts through the creases of her armor and had even made a couple of slashes on her face. Shaggy Dog fought savagely moving in a circle around her but could see the Princess was tiring out.

"Put on the Helm," he growled.

"I can't stop! There are too many," yelled the Princess.

"We need a new plan! Their numbers are too great," replied Shaggy Dog after sinking his teeth deep into the arm of a goblin attempting to strike high on the Princess's back. He backed in close to her as she reached down for the Helm.

As soon as it was snug on her head, she commanded, "Follow me, and keep them off my back for just a moment."

"Done!" barked Shaggy Dog after he tore into the thigh of another enemy. The Princess dug into the pouch at her waist and pulled out a small vial. She hesitated for just a second, then drained the contents into her mouth.

"Get behind me!" she yelled to Shaggy Dog.

He had barely made it before the Princess opened her mouth and fire billowed out. All of the nearby goblins were consumed, and the rest fled at the sight of the amber and crimson dragon's fire. Shaggy Dog stared in amazement at the Princess, who stood before their enemies and pushed them back defiantly with a weapon that was at once powerful but undoubtably painful to use. Then he saw her sway and fall to the ground from exhaustion. He called her name and licked her face, but she did not respond. He could see her chest rise and fall, so he knew she still lived. None of her wounds appeared to be serious, and the goblins were halfway to the northern mountains by now.

Shaggy Dog stood watch all night without a meal or a fire as the Princess rested.

Birds sang a morning serenade as the soft sunlight crested over the mountains in the east. Shaggy Dog could feel a light north wind dancing across his fur as he stretched out the stiffness of the night. Suddenly, his eyes snapped open, and he looked about frantically for the Princess.

Then Shaggy Dog's shoulders relaxed and his fur settled back down as he saw her lying in the same spot he had left her the night before. Her eyes were open and a small smile warmed her face as she greeted him.

"Good morning, sleepy head," she teased.

"Morning, Princess. How are you today? Do you hurt anywhere? Are you injured? Can you move?" blurted Shaggy Dog, each question rolling into the next.

"Slow down, my champion" laughed the Princess as she nuzzled her face against Shaggy Dog's fluffy head. He seemed to want to inspect every cut and scrape at once, but until she was out of her armor it was impossible.

"I will not. Now, how do you feel?" he persisted.

"Like I was run over by a horse. No, two horses pulling a cart – a *heavy* cart," she replied weakly. "But I don't think there's any permanent damage. Just tired and sore."

"Well, I'd expect so. You were amazing yesterday," said Shaggy Dog, settling down near the Princess. "Where did you learn to use that sword?"

"When Mom – I mean the Queen – is busy with court or some other obligation, I could sometimes sneak to the drill yard. If old Sergeant Rivers wasn't busy, he'd show me some things. Sergeant Gilbert actually let me run through exercises," she said dreamily. After a lengthy pause, she added, "It seems so long ago."

Shaggy Dog raised his head. "What does, Princess?"

The Princess let out a long sigh as she sat up. She gazed to the south, where she knew waves would now be crashing into the pink, sandy beach outside the castle she called home. Her mother would be doing important work for the people of Crystal Forge within those walls.

Long moments stretched out until she continued, "A normal life. As normal as a princess can have, anyway."

Shaggy Dog did not know what to say, so he remained silent. The sun was fully up, and the light dew on the grass was quickly being burned away. The breeze from the north had died down, and the whole world was still. They were both trapped within their own thoughts for the rest of the morning.

Around lunchtime, Shaggy Dog decided to go and fill their dwindling canteen from the stream. The Princess was skeptical but, after some creative maneuvering and strapping, Shaggy Dog set off toward the only nearby source of water with the canteen dangling from his neck. After a small meal and several more trips for Shaggy Dog to fill the canteen again and again, the Princess started to feel stronger. They chatted back and forth about nothing, or at least they specifically avoided discussing the previous day's attack. The next few days were spent this way: Shaggy Dog getting water and the duo eating small meals while conversing about nothing and anything as long as they avoided that particular subject. The Princess slowly recovered, and Shaggy Dog felt the need to resume their search for the canyon. Neither spoke about it, and all was peaceful.

The next day, without any chilly gusts of wind or the sound of thunder rattling in the distance, it started to rain. It was not a spring shower bringing life-refreshing water, and it was not even a fierce summer thunderstorm to cool the land. To Shaggy Dog it seemed like standing under a waterfall and getting pummeled. The Princess could not see five feet in front of her as her horse plodded slowly along, unsure of its footing. It rained for hours, and their progress was minimal. Shaggy Dog struggled tremendously through the muck as they crested a small rise. The Princess hopped down from her saddle, her boots making little splashes as they sank into the mud. As quickly as she could, she rummaged through the packhorse's burden, rearranging as she went. She examined her work from several angles as a dripping Shaggy Dog looked on. She had arranged the packs to support the small camp tabletop in the center. Then pushing down on the table, she created a nest-like structure. Shaggy Dog looked skeptical but remained silent.

"Now you can ride the pack horse," she said.

"Me? Ride a horse? That's ridiculous," scoffed Shaggy Dog. "How would I even get up there?"

"Well..."

"Why would I *want* to get up there?" complained Shaggy Dog.

"So we can make better time! You have to be exhausted sloshing through this stuff," said the Princess matter-of-factly.

"Oh! *I'm* slowing us down? Not as much as this stop is!"

With that, Shaggy Dog marched down the slippery slope, heading east. He made it to the bottom by sliding the last twenty feet on his face. He didn't even take his face out of the mud as the Princess plodded up to stand next to him, but said, "Any ideas how I can get on the platform?"

The duo endured the rain for several more hours. It never slacked off or showed any signs of doing anything but attempt to turn the whole of Crystal Forge into a lake. The Princess could hear Shaggy Dog muttering constantly about "frog-strangling rain" and how they would "need a boat or fins" before too long. She even heard him mumble something about what a "good mucking job" his horse was doing. Dark would come early on a day such as this, so it was no surprise when Shaggy Dog told the Princess they were stopping.

"I know of some rocks just to the south that might offer some protection," Shaggy Dog yelled over the constant thrum of the rain.

"And how would you know that?"

"I haven't lived at or near Seascape my whole life. It might surprise you, Princess, the places I have been and people I know," grumbled Shaggy Dog.

As they approached the rocks Shaggy Dog had mentioned, the Princess saw a sign directing travelers to something called the Ruff Gaming Tavern. Shaggy Dog was pointedly not looking anywhere near the sign as they passed it. Then the Princess noticed a small cave. They both agreed that a dirty and dry cave was better than a muddy and wet anything else.

After getting the horses unsaddled and picketed near the mouth of the cave, the duo was shocked to hear someone call out from deeper within.

"I suppose this cave is big enough for all of us," came a cheerful shout.

The Princess nearly jumped out of her armor, but Shaggy Dog crouched low, the hair on his neck bristling.

"No need in all that, friend-dog! I mean you no harm," continued the voice. "I am going to step forward. Don't bite me, now."

The Princess watched as a man barely taller than herself came around the corner. He was portly, with a long blue and white robe. His hands were extended and open, and there was a wide smile on his face. Shaggy Dog's posture relaxed and his tail swished involuntarily.

"See, it's just old trader Mikaela seeking refuge from the deluge. Much like yourselves, I would presume," continued the man as he walked into the failing light.

"That we are Michael-ah," said the Princess.

"The name is Mikaela, my dear. Both of you are soaked to the bone. Just around the corner I have a nice little camp with a fire, where I am cooking up a delectable stew. Come, get warm." He beckoned for them to follow him.

The thought of being warm and dry overpowered any reservations or suspicions. Around the bend in the tunnel, the cave opened up more than the outside view would lead one to believe possible. Shaggy Dog was glad to see the peddler had been truthful about the fire. As he and the Princess warmed themselves near it, Mikaela put the finishing touches on their supper.

After the small but delicious meal, Mikaela got straight to business. "Since I am such a gracious host, providing both a warm fire and a hot meal, I think it is time for you two to return the favor," he said with a glimmer in his eyes.

Until Mikaela spoke, Shaggy Dog had been sprawled out by the fire, feeling fat and happy. Now his ears lay flat and a quiet, deep growl rumbled in his chest.

"Calm down, Shaggy Dog," whispered the Princess. Then she spoke firmly to the peddler. "What do you have in mind, kind sir? For we can spare little to repay you."

"I seek nothing for free, my dear. I only wish to practice my craft," said the jolly little peddler. He laughed and continued, "You have given me no names, and I have not probed. It is obvious to anyone with eyes that you are on an important quest. Why else would you be out in this weather with such fancy armor and such a fine sword?"

"We *are* on a quest," stated the Princess, "and, as I have already mentioned, we have little with which to barter."

Shaggy Dog had resumed his lounging and was only half-listening. Trading and deal-making did not interest him in the least. Mikaela walked to the far side of the cave and rummaged through his packs. He returned with a sack, within which jostled a number of items.

"Well, let me show you the goods I can offer, then maybe you can think of something to part with," pushed Mikaela. "Maybe the dog's fancy collar? It is of giant origin, is it not?"

"It is not on the trading block, peddler," growled Shaggy Dog from beside the fire.

Mikaela's eyes grew wide and his mouth was agape. Then he bellowed a hearty laugh. "He speaks! I thought you were more than you let on. But I am correct? The collar you wear is of giant origin?"

"It was a gift from a friend," said the Princess. "And yes, he is a giant."

"I knew it! Ha. Not the giant's talisman, then. How about your sword or your armor? Surely with such a fearsome and loyal companion these are of no real use to you?"

The Princess sighed. "I wish you were right, Mr. Peddler, but I have great need of these items."

The peddler's grin slipped for just a moment, but then returned swiftly. "I mentioned my goods before, and here are some items I think you will appreciate. Perhaps after seeing them, you can think of something to trade."

First, Mikaela produced an ingenious saddle device. It had a retractable ramp that folded away underneath a flat, padded seat. He said it had once belonged to a rich prince who had enjoyed riding beside his prized dwarf pig. The pig would waddle up the ramp to sit in his saddle on his own horse. Then the ramp would be folded and stowed under the seat. It would be a serious upgrade for Shaggy Dog. A pleasant aroma assaulted the Princess's nose before the next item was even taken out of the bag. Spiced melons from across the Jasmine Sea – her mother's favorite, although the Princess could not remember the Queen having had any in quite some time. The last item was a purplish ball of soft light in a jar. The Princess heard Shaggy Dog's cry of surprise and looked closer at the jar. The light was actually a tiny forest fairy buzzing excitedly within the large glass container.

"Peddler, why do you have a right to trade such a creature?" inquired Shaggy Dog through tight lips.

"This little fairy had a debt to pay and made a choice in her repayment," replied Mikaela solemnly.

"I don't think that is very nice," protested the Princess.

"Shhh, now..." said Shaggy Dog urgently. He stared intently at the jar for several long seconds. Finally, he said, "The fairy tells me the peddler's explanation is true."

"See, I am but a humble trader and speak nothing but truth," sang the little peddler.

"Still, I don't think it is right," said the Princess sulkily.

"Then let's make a trade so you can set her free! You can balance the scales of this imagined injustice quite easily," relied Mikaela. "And I am so glad you can hear her, friend dog. I was not certain you would be capable, with all that fur."

"I can hear her plain as I hear you. But my friend has already told you we have nothing of value we can spare," said Shaggy Dog, without removing his eyes from the fairy.

"Begging your forgiveness, Mr. Peddler. I need a moment with my friend," the Princess said as she pulled Shaggy Dog to one side.

The peddler hummed and whispered happy sounds to the fairy.

The Princess was convinced they should trade anything not absolutely necessary for the fairy. Shaggy Dog wanted to help but was doubtful they could produce anything from their packs valuable enough to satisfy the peddler.

The Princess dug through her bag, inspecting each item in turn.

"Mr. Peddler," she started.

"It's Mikaela, dear," he replied softly.

"Mikaela, then. Would you be interested in some fine silk clothing? I'm sure they would fetch a big price," the Princess said, holding up both of her remaining shirts.

"Although those appear to be fit for royalty and very expensive, I am sure, my clientele would not appreciate the material," said Mikaela.

"Alright. Well, how about this silver dagger?" the Princess inquired, holding up a petite knife.

"Where did you get that?" a puzzled Shaggy Dog exclaimed.

"Never you mind that, Shaggy Dog. Peddler? I mean Mikaela?"

"That is fine work. I think I recognize the craftsmanship. I know a man down south near the pink shores who produces similar weapons. But I am not really in the business of trading arms," said Mikaela.

"Well, other than that... unless you want a hunk of rock that our giant friend said tasted funny, I'm out of items!" exclaimed an exasperated Princess.

"Does your friend hail from the north side of the Dragon Spine?" inquired Mikaela seriously.

"He does. Why do you ask?" replied the Princess.

"No matter. It's a deal," said the peddler with a chuckle.

"What's a deal?" asked a confused Princess. Shaggy Dog tilted his head questioningly.

"I will trade for the funny-tasting rock, of course," replied Mikaela. "Giants love to snack on any rock, and if one tasted funny to your friend, it must be quite unusual. Unusual can mean valuable. I'll take it."

"For the forest fairy?" asked the Princess hopefully.

"Tiny gods, no. For everything I showed you," came the cheerful reply.

The Princess was shocked, but accepted the deal eagerly. They made their exchange, and after Mikaela had helped the Princess mount Shaggy Dog's new riding platform, he slipped off to bed down for the night. The Princess could hear him humming a jolly tune for a few minutes until high-pitched snores filled the cave. Shaggy Dog was still near the fire, talking quietly to the fairy.

"Does she want us to let her out now?" asked the Princess.

"No. She wants to ride east with us for a while. It will take her closer to home," said Shaggy Dog.

"Well, she doesn't have to stay cooped up in that jar," said the Princess.

"I know, and so does she," said Shaggy Dog. "She can actually slip out of the breathing hole in the top any time she wants."

"Then why didn't she ever escape?" asked the Princess.

"I get the feeling she was never the peddler's prisoner," said Shaggy Dog.

"Well, I'll be. This has been one strange day, Shaggy Dog," said the Princess.

"It sure has."

"Maybe Mikaela can point us towards the canyon," said the Princess hopefully.

"Jazzi – that's the fairy's name – says she has known Mikaela a long time, and he probably knows exactly where it is," said Shaggy Dog.

"Great! We can ask him first thing in the morning," said the Princess as she rolled into her sleeping blanket.

"Jazzi says he won't be here in the morning," stated Shaggy Dog. "Princess? Princess?"

But the Princess was fast asleep.

She woke early the next morning eager to ask Mikaela about the canyon, but he had disappeared along with all of his belongings. Outside the cave, the rain continued to fall.

Chapter 6

When Daniel paused, I said, "That liquid fire is bad to the bone!"

"What?" he asked over the constant thrum from the other side of the bar.

"I said that fire the princess used is bad to the bone."

"Yeah. Worked well on the goblins," he replied.

"Seemed to take its toll on her too, though," Brandee added.

I looked down at my glass, surprised it was still mostly full, and waved off another round. The TV was showing the post-post-game show, and the college kids were at the tipping point of drunken euphoria and sloshy hell.

"Every time she had to use it, it got worse," Daniel muttered.

"She made a lot of cool friends, though. Did she ever see them again?" asked Brandee.

"Yeah, that big fella and eagle lady elf would be handy in a fight," I added.

Daniel's mouth twitched upwards slightly, but his eyes remained void of any emotion. "The Princess saw her friends again, or at least most of them. At this point in the story, she isn't even finished meeting interesting people yet."

The waitresses were buzzing around, and Brandee scooted off to fill orders. As I watched Daniel push his half empty beer across the bar, I remembered my own drink. I sipped lightly and stared at the TV, waiting for him to continue the story. He watched Brandee as she poured drinks and then went back to her textbook for a moment. When she closed it with a sigh, he said, "You should keep studying instead of listening to me ramble."

"That's OK. This is way better than the stuff I normally hear from that side of the bar," she replied.

I laughed and winked at Brandee. Then I told Daniel, "She doesn't have to study anyway, not really. She's majoring in art. How hard can that be?"

She flipped a dirty bar rag at me, laughing as she squealed, "Shut up, Jake, or I'll cut you off."

"Art? Like drawing and painting?" asked Daniel.

"Art history. I love to draw, and all forms of art, really. Maybe, one day I'll work in an art museum or something," she replied.

Daniel stood up so quickly that the barstool teetered back, threatening to crash to the floor. By the time it had settled back in place, he was three-quarters of the way to the restroom.

Brandee's eyes were wide as she looked at me. "Did I say something wrong?"

"Maybe, but this dude is on edge. He's raw. Anything could be the wrong thing to him," I told her reassuringly.

She looked toward the bathrooms, then back at me. She bit her lower lip softly, then asked, "Do you think his little girl had cancer?"

"Yeah, or something just as brutal," I said.

Her shoulders sagged. She drew a deep breath and said, "Can you even imagine... You want another one?"

"Yeah, give me one more." Then, after a moment, I added, "And no, I can't imagine."

Brandee reached for the bottle. "How is Janie? She's thirteen, right?"

I nodded my head, smiling. "She is good, good. I don't see her as much as I'd like, but busy, ya know?"

Brandee motioned with her eyes to point out Daniel as he made his way back to his stool. Once seated, he didn't waste any time. "The story picks up from here. Things start to happen fast, but if you are bored..."

"Hell no!" I replied. "I want to know if she ever finds the canyon."

"Alright then," he said. His eyes drifted from me to Brandee, then to his hands. One was clenched tight, and the other massaged it gently. "Let's do this."

Chapter 7

Three days later, the group resumed their eastern trek on a soggy but sunny road. It would have been only two days, but a fainting spell had struck the Princess. The Helm's instructions set her right, or at least better, quickly. Shaggy Dog was eager to push forward after he saw the mountains finally starting to take shape. He could even make out the snow caps on the tallest of the peaks. Jazzi chose to stay in her jar – but without the lid attached – upon Shaggy Dog's new platform. The Princess followed behind on her horse, eager to find her true weapon in the canyon.

Immediately, it was evident that the land was sloping up. Every hill they crested had a much shorter descent on the other side. It was on one of these hills, during the morning of the second day after leaving the cave, that they spotted the enemy scouts. At first, Shaggy Dog wasn't sure he had seen anything at all on the next ridge to the north, perhaps just a flicker of movement out of the corner of his eye. It wasn't until Jazzi asked him why the huge flock of ravens was following them that he put it together. Creeping goblins dressed in natural colors were keeping pace with them to the north, while the ravens came in and out of sight to the south. The enemy knew their exact location. Later that night, after their evening meal, the Princess fell asleep quickly due to exhaustion. Shaggy Dog watched as she slept peacefully without her armor or sword.

He had started to nod off himself when suddenly his ears shot up. He had heard a twig snap nearby. *Just an animal*, he thought. Then a wolf howled loudly, much too close for comfort. Jazzi flew out of her jar and straight to his ear, and whispered, "Quiet now. Wait for the response."

Seconds later, another wolf howled, followed by a third.

"See, they are all to the west of us. If they were going to attack, we would already be surrounded. Get some sleep. I'll stand watch tonight."

"You're probably right," said Shaggy Dog as he shuffled near to the Princess to get some rest, but sleep was slow to come and fitful when it arrived.

Every day after that was the same. The Goat Head Sorcerer's minions kept close watch on them all day. The Princess's fatigue caused by the curse forced them to take more frequent and longer breaks. Every night the wolves howled to each other, or the Princess and Shaggy Dog heard goblins racing near their camp. No one was getting the rest they needed, and it was taking its toll. Minor arguments broke out over things that did not matter. Small talk was all but absent. The traveling was still intense and productive, but at night their camp was quiet and lonely.

The Ravens of Despair attacked without warning on the sixth day since they first saw the enemy scouts. The Princess thought the dark cloud above them could mean another round of rain, until the cloud started cawing and diving towards them. Jazzi was the first to react, flying quickly from her jar to the Princess's shoulder just as the first ravens swooped down to peck at her. She stayed near the Princess's head, protecting her eyes from the sharp beaks and claws. Shaggy Dog felt a wave of uselessness wash over him. He sat frozen on his platform, feeling sorry for himself at just how impossible their task truly seemed.

More ravens came, and then still more. The Princess was almost overwhelmed by the sheer number of feathered fiends that descended upon her. She squealed in pain as a raven nipped at the back of her neck in the gap between the Helm and her armor. The pained sound finally knocked Shaggy Dog out of his stupor.

"Ride!" he yelled, urging his mount toward a stand of trees ahead. The Princess and Jazzi followed quickly. The ravens swirled up into the sky to regroup and prepare for another assault.

Shaggy Dog stopped in the midst of the thickest part of the wood. The Ravens of Despair came at the Princess again, but between the dense limbs and Shaggy Dog's merciless jaws, they soon grew bored and drifted off to the south, cawing raucously as they flew.

The decision to call an early halt to the day's travel was an easy one. The Princess made a small fire while Shaggy Dog stood watch. Jazzi flitted off into the thicket to do whatever forest fairies do in an unfamiliar clump of trees. When she came back, she whispered something into Shaggy Dog's ear.

For the first time in ages, Shaggy Dog smiled. He rushed off after Jazzi, telling the Princess he would be right back. When he came strutting back into camp, he was dragging a loaded branch of temple berries. The Princess could not help but smile as well; temple berries were just the thing to sweeten the bland meal she was preparing. Smashed and stewed, the berries were a delicacy. The Princess was already starting to salivate.

"Thought these would be a good pick-me-up," said Shaggy Dog as Jazzi buzzed past his head. "Fine, fine. *Jazzi and I* thought these would be a good pick-me-up."

"I love them. They're almost warm enough," said the Princess as she stirred the berry paste. "I haven't had temple berry biscuits in such a long time," she continued as she lifted the pot from the fire.

Just before tipping the steaming, sweet goo onto the hard biscuits, the Princess slipped. Temple berry sauce flew everywhere but onto the plate.

"Arrgh! Be more careful," growled Shaggy Dog.

The Princess's eyes grew wide, and her lower lip started to tremble. "I'm so sorry," she said.

"Sorry? That's the first decent thing to eat in days, and you say sorry?" barked the flustered Shaggy Dog.

Tears now filled the Princess's eyes and spilled down her cheeks. "It was an accident," she cried as she tried to mop up any sauce that was salvageable.

"Just forget it. Eat your biscuits and get some rest. We need to make up for lost time tomorrow," growled Shaggy Dog as he stormed off through the trees.

The Princess hugged her knees to her chest and sobbed heavily. Jazzi sat quietly on her shoulder until the sun set, when the Princess had calmed a little. The Princess rolled into her sleeping blanket sore, hurt, and hungry. The Ravens of Despair had accomplished their goal well.

The next morning, the Princess was the last to stir. Shaggy Dog had been up before dawn, scouring the area for something sweet for the Princess. He felt terrible about his reaction to the Princess's dropping of the temple berry sauce, and hoped to find something to help make it up to her. Jazzi stirred as the first light crept over the mountains, the same as she did every morning. Both waited anxiously for the Princess to rise from her slumber, eager to be on the road and away from this miserable place. Though the Ravens of Despair had not returned, the forlorn feeling they invoked had remained in the air like a wispy fog.

When the Princess finally stirred, she felt groggy and out of sorts. At Shaggy Dog's behest, she placed the Helm upon her head to try and find a solution. She dug in her pouch for a tiny clear vial. Almost instantly after drinking its contents, her head cleared slightly. Within the hour, she felt she was up to traveling, so the group struck out east, Shaggy Dog and Jazzi leading the way. Unfortunately, the Princess found herself digging back into the pouch again shortly after their midday meal.

For the next two days, as they traveled east with the mountains looming over them, the Princess used more vials and yet her condition became worse in spite of them.

The group started ascending the first foothills of the Dragon Spine Mountains, and with the help of the Helm and the vials, the Princess was able to manage. However, *manage* was all she was doing. So, on the ninth day since they first saw the enemy scouts, when they discovered that the pass they sought was guarded by two massive trolls, the Princess felt like giving up and just going home. She couldn't have turned around even if she wanted to, though. Wolves had been following them all day, howling even in the daylight. The only way was forward.

They crested a small rise onto a flat plateau. To their right was a steep drop into a nasty-looking swamp. To their left was a vertical ridge towering above them. The wolves, their numbers impossible to discern, howled closer behind them. As Shaggy Dog looked out across the elevated plain, dread filled his heart. Up ahead, blocking the only other way to the mountains and eventually the canyon, was a small army of goblins lined in formation. Shaggy Dog did not bother to count them, as their numbers were too great to matter whether there were eighty or one hundred and twenty.

He heard the Princess moan. "So many," she said.

"Yes, but look," said Shaggy Dog with a wolfish grin. "They are scared to attack. Word of the fire-breathing Princess Knight, menace to all goblins, must have reached them."

Despite herself and despite their dire situation, the Princess giggled. *It feels good to laugh*, she thought as she loosened the sword in its scabbard.

As Jazzi buzzed past her face and towards the swamp, the Princess said, "Where is she going?"

"She didn't say, only something about time," replied Shaggy Dog without taking his eyes from the goblins.

"Little Jazzi couldn't fight these things anyway," said the Princess, looking towards the murky swamp into which Jazzi had plunged. It was probably a better place to be than here with the goblins. "No time like the present," she continued as she urged her horse forward.

Shaggy Dog could see some of the goblins unsheathe their swords and loosen their axes at the sight of the Princess moving towards them, but they held their position.

"Whoa now, Princess," said Shaggy Dog sternly.

"Whoa yourself! What are we waiting for? A miracle?" screamed the Princess. "No, let's be done with this."

Shaggy Dog angled his mount in front of hers and looked her dead in the eye. "Don't go rushing to your death. Hear me out."

The Princess simply nodded, so Shaggy Dog continued, "Here, we have some high ground. The goblins know that, which is why they haven't attacked yet. Smarter than most people give them credit for. And besides, Jazzi squealed something about time, or more time, on her way past us. Let's not rush. We'll have our fight at some point today."

The Princess looked away, then stared at the goblins for a long time. Finally, she looked back at Shaggy Dog. "Fine, we make our stand here."

The sun was almost at its highest point, and the unseasonable warm weather had the Princess reaching for her canteen after only minutes had passed. Still, they waited on the hillside, standing upright in defiance of their fear. Shaggy Dog watched as the Princess stared out at an enemy bent on her destruction. She did not flinch or shy away. He realized how proud he was of her bravery and spirit. After a moment of weakness, she was no longer consumed by fear or intimidated by the odds. She was truly a noble warrior.

The sun passed the midday point and was well into its descent when the goblin army started its slow march forward. The Princess spared a single glance towards the swamp, hoping to see Jazzi returning. She had grown fond of the little fairy in the last few days. But no, it appeared that the Princess and Shaggy Dog would face this threat alone.

The Princess pulled her sword from her scabbard, and the orderly march of the goblins crumbled into an all-out riot racing towards them. A group of ten, perhaps twelve of the fastest goblins outpaced the main group. They were lightly armored with short, thin swords. Their battle cry rang across the plateau as they came within thirty paces of the Princess and Shaggy Dog, who were both still on their horses. They waited stoically with the Princess slightly ahead of Shaggy Dog, grasping her sword loosely.

"We will only have a few moments to dispense with the first wave before the main force is upon us," said Shaggy Dog calmly. "Whatever you do, stay on your horse."

"Are you going to stay on yours?" asked the Princess. Shaggy Dog smiled his wolfish smile again, showing his large teeth, and laughed.

"Guess not," said the Princess.

And then the goblins were upon them.

Shaggy Dog barked, "Now! Back!"

Quickly, the Princess pulled her horse back a few steps as Shaggy Dog urged his forward ahead of the Princess. Solely focused on the Princess as they were, half the goblins were ridden down by Shaggy Dog's horse. The remainder were forced to slow down and maneuver around the results of the carnage. Now the goblins had lost their best tactical advantage: speed. The five remaining goblins regrouped and attacked the Princess's unprotected side. Shaggy Dog watched as she worked the reins deftly with one hand and wielded her sword in the other. The Princess never allowed more than one goblin forward at a time and dispatched each one efficiently. When she wrenched the sword free from the last one, she looked up, expecting to see the main force bearing down on them.

"Why do they wait?" asked the Princess, breathing heavily.

"I don't know. They're within bow range, but I don't see any archers," replied Shaggy Dog. "You did well, by the way."

"And you are still on your horse!" mocked the Princess.

"There was no reason to get down. You had it covered," he said, glancing at her.

"We're not done yet," she said. Then, more loudly, "What are you waiting for?!"

There was a ripple through the lines of the goblin army, creating a gap in the center. The ground shook as a huge troll stormed through the gap to the front of the line. It paused and roared a challenging battle cry to the Princess. Shaggy Dog's mouth hung open as he stared, but without hesitation, the Princess raised her sword high in the air and answered in kind. The next instant, the troll charged. The Princess leveled her sword like a lance and spurred her horse forward, Shaggy Dog right at her heels. The clash reverberated in Shaggy Dog's chest as the Princess's sword shattered against the troll's extended, meaty fist. The troll went down, grasping his ruined hand as the Princess flew from her saddle, landing hard on the unforgiving ground. Shaggy Dog positioned himself between the troll and the Princess as she slowly regained her feet. She swayed as she reached into the pouch, searching for a vial of Dragon's Fire. The troll had struggled to his feet and thrust his bloody fist at Shaggy Dog.

"Move, Shaggy Dog!" yelled the Princess as she tossed the handle of her bladeless sword to the ground. She turned up the vial and drank the bitter liquid quickly.

"As you command," said Shaggy Dog, maneuvering his horse behind her.

The troll charged, malice in his eyes and foam coming from his mouth. When it was only feet away from her, the Princess released the fire deep from within. Her eyes were bloodshot and full of tears, and her whole body shook from the strain.

The troll was engulfed by the searing flame, but it still raised his undamaged fist high to smash the Princess like a bug. The Princess continued to spew flame even as she fell to her knees. The troll staggered one more step, then fell with a bone-rattling crash. Shaggy Dog let out a whoop from up on his horse... but it died out when he noticed the goblins advancing with swords, tiny pikes, and axes drawn. The Princess was still on her knees with her head lowered and her arms dangling listlessly.

The Princess did not stir as the goblins started their advance. As they realized she was not going to repeat the dragon's fire, their pace increased. Something within

Shaggy Dog snapped; his ears lay flat on his head as he sprang from the platform into the first unlucky goblin. Before its blood hit the ground, Shaggy Dog was upon another goblin, then another. Vaguely, he was aware that the Princess was struggling to stand, and that she was grasping the small, silver knife. His vision was dark around the edges as he ripped and gnashed goblin after goblin. Blood was everywhere, and he was pretty sure some of it was his, but he was positive that none of it belonged to the Princess. The goblins pulled back in the face of his ferocity, and the Princess staggered over and placed a hand on his heaving back. The red ground was littered with goblin bodies, but there were still too many amassing to charge again.

"Stay behind me, Princess. They won't touch you," gasped Shaggy Dog.

The Princess was too weary to argue that once they were surrounded it would all be over. The goblins were spreading into a half-moon shape, in order to accomplish just that, when Jazzi landed on the Princess's shoulder. She kissed the Princess's cheek lightly, then buzzed down to Shaggy Dog.

"What?" growled Shaggy Dog. Jazzi gestured with both hands towards the swamp. "Will that work? Can you do it?"

Frantically, he glanced from side to side, then saw what he was looking for. "Fine, but you'd better be right!"

"Be right about what?" asked the Princess.

"No time. Jazzi has a plan. When they attack, stay very close," Shaggy Dog replied, still scanning the goblins assembling between them and the swamp.

"I will, but what's the plan?" whined the exhausted Princess.

"Just don't stop. Eliminate anything in our path, but for the tiny gods' sake, don't stop," growled Shaggy Dog.

Jazzi buzzed off towards the swamp again, moments before the goblins charged. Shaggy Dog didn't hesitate: immediately, he sprinted in the direction Jazzi had flown. The Princess saw six of the tallest, meanest-looking goblins she had ever seen right in front of them.

"Umm... Shaggy Dog, what are we doing?" yelled the Princess as she stumbled after him as fast as she could.

"Just keep moving," grunted Shaggy Dog as he approached the goblins.

Wicked, sharp teeth showed through the triumphant smiles of the largest goblins as Shaggy Dog and the Princess approached. An armorless mutt and a little girl with only a knife and no Dragon's Fire remaining would be no match for them. Swords raised, they charged or at least, they *tried* to charge. Vines had grown up around their ankles and tripped them up. They fell face first as the Princess and Shaggy Dog passed them on their way to the steep drop and the swamp. The other goblins saw they were through the lines and quickly pursued them. Suddenly, a wall of vines covered with thorns sprang out of the dirt, blocking the goblins from their pursuit. Shaggy Dog and Princess kept running right to the edge of the cliff

"Jump!" yelled Shaggy Dog.

"Are you crazy?" asked the Princess with wide eyes.

"Trust me. Jump."

As they sailed over the edge, the swamp raced up to meet them. Jazzi flew alongside them, leaving a little trail of fairy light behind her. Moments before they struck the tops of the trees, vines came shooting out of the canopy and wrapped gently around their bodies, bringing them slowly to the soft ground.

They had escaped the goblin army!

Jazzi buzzed around, checking their injuries, and Shaggy Dog let out a victorious howl to rival the loudest wolf. The Princess smiled at her friends, then sank slowly to her knees. She saw the bright afternoon sun fading as she slowly slipped into the delirium of dreams due to utter exhaustion.

A sandpaper tongue and a scorching pain in her throat were the first things the Princess noticed as she woke. The ground squished under her back and hands as she pushed herself up to a sitting position. The pleasant, damp smell of decay filled her nostrils as she scanned her surroundings. Thick moss hung from gnarled, ancient trees, dragging on the ground like overgrown beards. Sunlight cascaded through the few gaps in the thick branches. She felt warm and sweaty. Shaggy Dog and Jazzi were nowhere to be seen, and she decided maybe she didn't need to sit up after all. She stared at the interlocking limbs above her until her eyes slowly closed again.

The next time she swam out of the deep and opened her eyes it was still daylight, but noticeably dimmer. All she could see was a tangle of black hair and two big white eyes.

"Rise and shine, Princess," said Shaggy Dog quietly.

The Princess sat up with some effort as Shaggy Dog shuffled to one side gingerly.

"Are you hurt?" asked the Princess.

"I'll manage. I gave more than I got, that's for sure."

"Where is Jazzi?" asked the Princess, scanning the swamp around them.

"Flitting around, keeping the goblins out of this murky hole," said Shaggy Dog with a small grin. "She is quite amazing. The vine thing on the plateau was all her doing, and some of the things she is doing now is beyond my understanding. But it's keeping us safe, that much I know."

As the conversation lulled, the Princess drank deeply from her canteen. Animal sounds and the constant drone of insects were the only noises in the dense swamp. There was no breeze, and the Princess thought the air felt heavy and thick. "It's insufferable here – so hot," she said.

"Don't let Jazzi hear you say that," laughed Shaggy Dog. "When I think of forest fairies, I think of tall redwood glens or elegant willows on the banks of a winding river. But Jazzi says this swamp reminds her of home. She is more giddy than usual, so be prepared."

Shaggy Dog looked at the Princess out of the corner of his eye, and they both laughed quietly. The Princess continued to sip on her canteen, feeling her strength return slowly.

"Is there anything to eat?" she asked, doubtful that there would be.

"Jazzi pointed out some fluffy water-pad things she said were edible, if not good. But all of our supplies are up there with the horses, except for this one bag Jazzi was able to haul down here yesterday," said Shaggy Dog, looking at the single, pitiful bag that housed the two canteens, flint, and hard cheeses.

"Wait – yesterday?" asked a puzzled Princess. "How long have I been asleep?"

"Well, if you don't count the day we launched ourselves off the plateau," said Shaggy Dog cautiously, "four days."

"Four days!" exclaimed the Princess. She attempted to stand, without much success. "We need to be moving. We have to get out of here and into the canyon!"

Shaggy Dog nudged her gently back down to a wet landing. He cocked his head to the side and looked at her.

"I guess maybe we can rest a bit more," said the Princess. "Just till Jazzi gets back."

Jazzi did not return that day or even that night. When the Princess was roused by Shaggy Dog shortly after dawn the next morning, Jazzi was zooming from side to side and back and forth so quickly that the Princess struggled to keep track of her. The Princess saw Shaggy Dog's furled brow, flat ears, and straight tail as he tried to get the little fairy to slow down.

"Jazzi, just stop, or at least fly in a small circle so we can talk," said Shaggy Dog as Jazzi flew by them again.

"What's wrong with her?" asked the Princess as she approached Shaggy Dog.

"I can't tell. She's not making a lot of sense," he whispered.

Then Jazzi stopped and flew right onto Shaggy Dog's nose. The Princess giggled as Jazzi pointed her tiny finger at his eye, obviously giving him the once-over. Shaggy Dog cleared his throat and, never taking his eyes off the little fairy still perched on his snout, continued, "Correction: Jazzi says she is making perfect sense. Evidently, I am just a dumb, hard of hearing... dog."

Immediately, Jazzi started jabbing her finger at him again and stamping her foot impatiently.

"I am *not* saying that in front of her..." Shaggy Dog said. Then, after a pause, "Alright, I am an oaf, a dumb oaf. Is that better?"

It must have been more to the fairy's liking because Jazzi resumed her pacing like a hummingbird flittering from flower to flower. Shaggy Dog explained to the Princess that Jazzi had said there was something very wrong with this swamp. She did not know what exactly, but she could not seem to find a way out. She flew due south for one solid day, yet ended up where she started. She waited for goblins to enter the swamp looking for the Princess, and after dispatching them, she followed their trail backwards. The trail simply vanished. When she flew far enough above the canopy, she could see the edge, but once back down here, it disappeared.

"See, she isn't making any sense," mumbled Shaggy Dog as he looked at Jazzi out of the corner of his eye. Then, he sighed deeply when she did not hear him.

"We don't have a choice. We have to get out of this swamp," said the Princess. "I say we walk east – that's the way we were going anyway."

After a meal of spongy water pads, the group started their trudge east. Shaggy Dog missed his horse and platform with every paw-sucking step, and progress was slow. Nevertheless, they were moving again, and the Princess felt better knowing that the goblins could not reach them in here. The prospect of leaving the swamp to continue the search for the canyon was too far off to bother her at the moment. She concentrated on putting one foot in front of the other and not falling into the muck.

When they finally stopped that night, Shaggy Dog and the Princess were exhausted. Jazzi went out scouting and came back to report that the goblins had given up on entering the swamp, but she still did not know how to get out.

The next morning started just as the last evening had ended: mud, muck, slow moving, and frustration with no end in sight. The Princess, in particular, started to lose her cool after a root she hadn't noticed sent her sprawling on the runny ground. She had mud all along her front, on her face, and in her hair. If anyone had been standing on the plateau above, they would have heard her scream of annoyance. When Shaggy Dog plopped over to help, she screamed at him too. Her eyes were wide with rage as she kicked at every plant, stick, and root within reach. She took out her knife and threw it at a swamp rat scurrying past. Luckily for the rat, her anger caused her aim to be off, which only elevated the temperature of her blood until she boiled over. She picked up a hunk of dead wood and was about to chunk it into a tree when she saw Shaggy Dog's slack-jawed expression.

She deflated, and fell back onto the squishy ground. Her tears mixed with the swamp water as her whole body was racked with sobs. She looked at Shaggy Dog after her tears had mostly dried up. She saw only love and worry. He was not angry at her for her outburst. She knew in that moment that rage was not going to carry her through to the end of her quest, or even to the end of this swamp. Rage was not her weapon.

The next morning offered more of the same mud and muck. Shaggy Dog pointed out a particularly odd-looking bent cypress tree, which he thought looked like an old dried-out raider wraith. It was spooky but extremely interesting, a rarity during their monotonous grind. The Princess was tired of eating the water pads and longed for something hot and filling. Shaggy Dog never complained, but on several occasions, he did ask Jazzi where the nearest inn could be found.

Nothing changed until Shaggy Dog stopped dead in his tracks, staring out at the swamp. He said, "It has to be the same one."

Jazzi left the Princess's shoulder to buzz around near Shaggy Dog's head.

"The same what?" asked the Princess.

"There – right there," Shaggy Dog said, pointing with his nose to the right.

The Princess peered in that direction but all she saw were trees and vines and swamp. She was just about to tell Shaggy Dog so when she saw a familiar shape. It was like an old dried-out raider wraith, but it was just a tree. The tree they had passed hours earlier.

The hairs on the back of Shaggy Dog's neck stood up and his eyes narrowed. He stalked over to the tree with large, careful steps. After walking around it and inspecting it from all angles, he returned to the group.

"It's just a tree," he said through gritted teeth.

"Shaggy Dog, are you alright?" asked the Princess, reaching out with one hand to settle the fur on his back.

"I'm fine, just angry. I'm mad at the whole thing, from this swamp all the way back to the Goat Head Sorcerer," he said, calming as he spoke. "Sometimes the anger is all that drives me, but it bubbled over just now. I thought that tree was some kind of sign, since we have already seen it once – or maybe whatever has trapped us here was near to it. But nobody was there, and it's just a tree."

"Just a tree," repeated the Princess.

Jazzi flew onto Shaggy Dog's nose and her speech became very animated, her tiny arms going everywhere as she talked.

"Jazzi says the swamp just told her of another presence nearby. Not goblins, but the swamp doesn't recognize it either," said Shaggy Dog.

"Well, let's go have a look, shall we?" said the Princess.

Shaggy Dog just shook his head quietly, laughing. "Nothing seems to bother you – well, other than that root back there. But seriously, you are handling this so well."

"I just have faith. Faith that we are on the right path set forth by the Benevolent Witch. Faith in those that have helped me. The Queen gave me this armor. Reserio and the witches of Houstonia gave me the Helm and sword, although the sword is gone. Sasha and Dane gave us useful gifts: wisdom and friendship. Even Mikaela gave us Jazzi, and look how wonderful she is." The Princess nudged the little fairy with her pinky finger. "It's all going to work out, one way or another. I just know it."

"I hope you are right..." Shaggy Dog said. Then he cocked his head. "What, Jazzi?" He listened intently to the fairy for a moment, then stared straight ahead. "Are you sure? I don't see anything. Of course you are. Princess, get behind me. The weird presence thing in the swamp is almost on top of us."

The Princess stepped behind Shaggy Dog and looked intently into the dense swamp. She could hear the presence long before she could see it. It was definitely coming straight for them, and making a terrible racket.

Then she could barely believe her ears.

"Shaggy Dog, is someone singing?" she asked quietly.

"I think so. Something about a fish on a hook wiggling loose. A nonsense children's song," replied Shaggy Dog, relaxing a bit. He recognized the voice.

The owner of the voice struggled through the foliage, splashing right up to them. The Benevolent Witch had returned.

"Well, hello Princess, Shaggy Dog," she said in her high-pitched voice. "And who might you be, little one?"

The Benevolent Witch listened intently to the fairy, then giggled aloud, "What a lovely name – Jazzi! I see you have met my friends, and helped them along, I suspect."

Shaggy Dog was staring at the Benevolent Witch like as if she was an aberration that he could not quite comprehend. The Princess was the first to speak up. "Madam Witch, it's great to see you. But what are you doing here?"

The Benevolent Witch giggled again. "Didn't I tell you I would meet you again at the canyon? I did, didn't I? Well, either way, you all are here, and Princess, you have completed the tests. So, I am here."

"Tests? What tests?" asked a thoroughly confused Princess. "And what do you mean, we are in the canyon? We're right in front of you in this smelly swamp."

"Ah, I see. That is strange. You have completed the tests and the illusion has still not passed? Very strange," said the Benevolent Witch. "Well, where is your sword? I want to see it."

"I am so confused. I haven't found any sword in this swamp," cried the Princess.

"But you have found your weapon. The tests are complete – the canyon tells me this is so," stated the Benevolent Witch matter-of-factly.

The Princess threw her hands up and laughed. She walked over to the old crooked tree and leaned very close, almost touching it. Finally, without knowing what else to do, she closed her eyes and whispered softly to the tree.

"I have faith, old tree. I have faith that however this will end, those around me, love me. I have faith that the world is a good place filled with good creatures. I have faith for the future." By the end of her statement, her lips were touching the bark of the bent old tree. When she opened her eyes, she saw a hole in the tree she was sure hadn't been there moments ago. Without hesitation, she reached in and grasped the handle of a sword.

Shaggy Dog's eyes grew wide as the Princess pulled from within the tree a small, beautiful glass sword. It had a silver rod at its core running the length of the blade from pommel to tip. As the Princess returned to the group, he could see the word *Faith* written on the core. She had found her weapon and with it, her chance to defeat the Goat Head Sorcerer once and for all.

The Benevolent Witch's laughter rang across the swamp. A haze filled the air, and then swamp faded slowly, like fog being burned by a bright morning sun escaping the clouds. The group found themselves in a deep narrow canyon: *the* Canyon. They had been there all along.

Jazzi chattered away, but Shaggy Dog was not paying attention. All he could see was the defiant smile on the Princess's face. She was ready for the challenge ahead; he just knew it.

The sky was quickly becoming muted, as night fell quickly in the canyon. The group, the Benevolent Witch included, decided to camp where they were for the night. Having a witch around paid off: she provided warm food for the group for the first time in days. They ate until they could not stomach another bite. Then, they ate some more. Anything was better than the fluffy water pads that had sustained them in the swamp. Sleep came upon the Princess hard, but Shaggy Dog was restless. He wandered around the camp, finally settling down near the Benevolent Witch.

"Go ahead and ask me," she said.

Jazzi heard the Benevolent Witch talking to Shaggy Dog and buzzed over, interested.

"Alright, what do we do next?" asked Shaggy Dog.

"I honestly do not have a good answer for you," said the Benevolent Witch in an uncharacteristically melancholy tone. "The results of her skirmishes with the minions of the Goat Head Sorcerer are encouraging. But she seems so tired."

Shaggy Dog agreed that the Princess looked tired, and that she was hurting more than she let on. He pressed on. "But she has her true weapon now. What is the next move?"

The Benevolent Witch sighed deeply, looking first at the fairy and then at Shaggy Dog. "I think she should rest. Maybe even go home for a bit before she has to confront him. If she does it now, I fear she will not be strong enough, weapon or no weapon."

An uncomfortable silence fell across the group. The Princess lay just feet away, sleeping soundly and getting the rest she so needed and deserved. Smoke from the little fire blew into Shaggy Dog's eyes, so he got up to move.

"Don't lose heart, Shaggy Dog," said the Benevolent Witch. "She will need you in the end."

Shaggy Dog just nodded and lay down next to the Princess. However, sleep was a long time coming that night.

The next morning, Jazzi informed the others that she was ready to return to her home swamp. It would not be a long flight, and she was eager to see her family. The Princess and Shaggy Dog both thanked her for her tremendous efforts. In turn, Jazzi thanked them for helping free her from the peddler, laughing as she said it. The Benevolent Witch also departed that morning, but not before telling them where she believed they could locate their horses, if they chose to do so.

The Princess and Shaggy Dog found themselves alone on their quest again. This time, however, it was much different. They had the Princess's true weapon and had proven that the minions of the Goat Head Sorcerer were not unbeatable. Hope grew in Shaggy Dog's heart. The Princess did not have room for hope; she still fought every day to put one foot in front of the other and to soldier on. The curse was making it tougher each day.

Shortly after their midday meal, the duo started the trek out of the canyon. Shaggy Dog led the way around strewn boulders and through cracks and fissures. They talked quietly, debating their best course of action. Neither of them had any inspired ideas, so the conversation went in circles. They rounded a sharp bend in the narrow, high canyon to see a flat expanse in front of them. A brisk wind blew on their backs as they started across the plain. The Princess realized they were much higher up in the mountains than she had thought. The swamp, which was really the canyon, was trickier than she had ever imagined. The air was chilly even beneath her armor, but at least there were no signs of goblins or trolls. The duo did not even see a single raven as they crossed the high, flat land.

With several hours of daylight left, Shaggy Dog and the Princess arrived at the little valley in which their horses could be found, if the Benevolent Witch was correct. The valley was more colorful than anything they had seen in weeks. The leaves on the giant trees were all the colors of the rainbow, from orange to red, and even green and blue and more. The Princess stopped and gazed at their beauty for a long time. Shaggy Dog stopped as well, but all he could see was a bunch of trees and no horses.

"Do you see them, Princess?" he asked, without any real hope.

"Oh yes. They're beautiful," exclaimed the Princess. "We never see trees with this much color at home. Flowers, yes, but not whole trees."

Shaggy Dog smiled and rolled his eyes, his tail swishing from side to side. "Not the leaves, for the tiny gods' sake. Do you see the horses? You know, the big, white animals we're looking for?"

They both laughed, and Shaggy Dog leaned against the Princess. *It really is a spectacular view,* he thought.

Shoulders back and jaw set, the Princess said, "That's it."

"What's what?"

"When this is all over, I know what I want to do," she said.

Shaggy Dog's ears raised and his tail moved faster. "And what is that, Princess?"

She didn't take her eyes off the trees as she replied, "I am going to learn to paint. Then, I will visit all the beautiful places in the Forge in order to paint them."

The Princess looked at Shaggy Dog with wide eyes. He looked back with his wolfish grin and said, "And all this time I thought you were going to be a knight."

"No. The drill yard is fine for me, thank you very much," the Princess said. "I've had enough fighting, even though we're not through yet. I think I'd like to paint so that others can at least glimpse the beauty of the Forge even if they can't see it for themselves."

They stood looking at the leaves. The Princess was picking out her favorite colors while Shaggy Dog was thinking how amazing she was. Despite all that the world and the Goat Head Sorcerer had thrown at her, she still saw the beauty and wanted nothing more than to share it with others.

"Well, we need to find those horses," said the Princess abruptly.

"We do. Let's go." Shaggy Dog started down into the valley, eager to find the horses, but then he felt the Princess's hand on his back.

"Not that way," she said. "Let's climb that ridge. If they're here, we'll spot them from up there."

Shaggy Dog nodded and bowed deep. "Lead the way, Your Majesty."

Sasha would have been proud of them if she could have seen how well they managed to follow the game trail up the side of the ridge. The footing was sure, and the path consistent. When Shaggy Dog let out a yelp of pain as he slipped backwards several feet, the Princess was shocked. She went to his side quickly. Shaggy Dog had been watching an eagle on the horizon, thinking about their last encounter with an eagle, when he had stepped on a loose rock that had slid out from under him. His front paw was bent at an awkward angle and already showed significant swelling. *Broken, for sure*, he thought as he struggled to rise. The pain sent him back to the ground. He hopped the last fifteen feet up the ridge with the Princess directly behind him in case he faltered. Once at the top, Shaggy Dog flopped down in a heap, exhausted and in pain. The Princess started to examine his paw but he snapped, "Look for the horses before we lose the light!"

"Just let me examine your paw," said the Princess.

"The horses!" growled Shaggy Dog.

The Princess recoiled, the shock plain on her pale face.

"I'm so sorry, Princess," said Shaggy Dog, rearranging himself to look her in the eyes. "I'm just mad at my own stupidity. I was birdwatching instead of paying attention to the trail. Idiot."

The Princess ruffled the fur on his head as she stood. "Let me look for the horses. Then you're going to let me check on at that paw."

The ridge offered an excellent view of the valley. The Princess could see trees, then a small stream that cut the valley in half. She could see clear across to the other side where the mountains rose again, steeper even than the ridge they were on. She did not see the horses, though, and was in the process of telling Shaggy Dog the bad news when she spotted something coming towards them.

"Is that the eagle you saw earlier?" she asked, pointing towards the rapidly growing winged creature.

"I think so," Shaggy Dog said, the hair on his back rising. He yelled, "Princess! That's no eagle. It's a dragon. We have to hide!"

"A dragon? Are you sure?" Even as she said it, she knew Shaggy Dog was right. The creature was huge, with a bright yellow belly, and there was no doubt that it was headed straight for them.

"Come on. The Goat Head Sorcerer could have sent it to find us. We have to move!" barked Shaggy Dog, struggling to move quickly towards a pile of rocks near the other end of the ridge.

"Where are we going to go?" cried the Princess as she pulled out her sword. "There's nowhere to hide."

The dragon passed over them at incredible speed. As it banked hard to come back towards them, the Princess saw that it had a dark green back that transitioned to a yellow belly. It swooped down close to their heads, the wind from its massive wings almost knocking the Princess off her feet. Quickly, it dropped to the ground lightly. A boy barely older than herself jumped off the dragon's back, deftly landing on his feet. There was a quiver on his back but no bow in sight. He approached with his hands raised.

"Hey now, don't stick me with that thing. It looks sharp," he said with a perfect smile.

The Princess looked down at her drawn sword, surprised to see it in her hands, but she did not lower it.

"Don't come any closer!" said the Princess, brandishing her sword.

With one hand, the boy indicated the lack of scabbard on his belt. "I don't carry a blade, and I left my bow back there with Zero."

"Your dragon has a name?" The Princess didn't know why, but she was intrigued by this piece of news.

"Of course. Doesn't your dog have a name?"

"I do," growled Shaggy Dog, limping up beside the Princess with his hackles raised. Zero stirred, but a slight gesture from the boy seemed to calm him.

The boy said sagely, "All of the tiny gods' creatures have names. Mine is Jaxson, and I – well, *we* –live one valley over. Zero spotted you and thought you might be goblins, so we came to investigate."

"Goblins? Have you seen any?" asked the Princess in concern.

"Not for weeks. They tend to give Zero plenty of space," Jaxson said with a chuckle.

Shaggy Dog had no choice: he had to sit down, and even that hurt.

"You are wounded. Why don't both of you come to our place? We'll get you all fixed up," offered Jaxson.

"I'm fine, boy," said Shaggy Dog defiantly. "Besides, how can we trust you? We don't even know you."

"Doesn't look like you have much choice. And if I meant either of you harm, I would have used my bow or let Zero have a crack at you. I just don't see many folks up this way. Kind of want to hear why you two are up here, and maybe some news of the world."

Shaggy Dog thought for a moment. "If you want to help us, get your dragon to fly around and find our horses. That would be *actual* help."

It was Jaxson's turn to look down at his hands, suddenly very quiet. "Two white horses?"

"So, you *have* seen them?" the Princess squealed with delight.

Jaxson blushed. "Yep. About three days ago. They were right down in that valley there." With a sweep of his hand, he indicated the valley they were all overlooking.

"Where? Can you show us?" she asked.

Shaggy Dog could see something was off, so he asked, "Where are the horses now?"

Jaxson gave a sheepish smile. "Well, one is probably halfway to Bent Pine by now. The other is at my place. Meat is hard to come by up here."

The Princess stared blankly at Jaxson. Understanding dawned upon her and her facial expression went through a range of emotions. All she said was, "That stinks."

"Guess we could use some help after all, boy," Shaggy Dog said gruffly. Jaxson's sheepish smile grew into a genuine face-splitter. He nodded and beckoned them towards Zero.

Chapter 8

"Excuse me. I'm so sorry to interrupt," came a sweet voice said from behind Daniel. The older lady from the end of the bar stood meekly right behind him. "We're leaving. Curt is too far in the cups. I just wanted to tell you I loved listening to your story and would love to hear the end some time."

Daniel just nodded as the woman smiled sadly and went to escort her inebriated partner through the door. The few remaining college kids were paying their tabs. I hadn't realized how late it was. Within minutes, we were alone: just me, Brandee, and Daniel.

"You gonna kick us out?" I asked her.

Brandee shrugged. "I'll lock up when I want to."

"Good. I'm gonna hit the head," I said, pushing myself away from the bar.

On my way back to my stool, I heard them discussing the Princess's weapon.

"Things were dark, but at least there was now a chance," Daniel said.

"Shaggy Dog didn't think so. He's giving up," I said as I sat on my stool.

Brandee's eyes grew large, and her hands stopped making a drink mid-pour. Daniel's next words were barely louder than a whisper. "What did you say?"

Brandee attempted to shush me with her hands, but I continued, "Shaggy Dog's feeling sorry for himself. He got mad over some spilled fruit earlier, and now he's being a jerk. Pitiful, really."

I saw Daniel's eyes come alive. There was no far-off gaze, and he seemed no longer trapped in a memory. Instead, his eyes became twin furnaces barely containing a fire within that promised to consume anything it touched. The hair on the back of my neck stood up, and I thought the big, bearded man was going to crush me.

Brandee came to my rescue by slapping my tab forcefully on the bar. "Sir, Jake here is paying your tab tonight," she said sternly.

Daniel didn't seem to hear her. His eyes remained focused on me, and I pulled back as he said, "You don't have a clue."

He stood and turned away. Without looking back, he crashed through the front door, leaving us behind. I kept my gaze on the dregs at the bottom of my glass, too fearful to meet Brandee's eyes. Just as my heart had resumed a semblance of its normal rhythm, I heard the front door open again. Daniel filled the doorway.

He said calmly, "I have to finish this story."

All I could see were his eyes. The fire was under control, but it was still there, smoldering.

He settled heavily into his seat and said, "I have to finish it. Not for you or you..." He pointed at me then Brandee as he continued, "Not even for me. I have to tell the end for *her*, because I don't think I'll ever be able to tell this story again. And it deserves to be told. She deserves to have it heard."

"Alright, then tell it, and I'll keep my flapper shut," I said.

Daniel nodded.

"Brandee, I know it's late, but can I get one more drink?" I asked.

"It's not late. It's early," she said absently, staring at Daniel. "But sure. Hell, I'll have one too."

Daniel waited on Brandee to finish pouring our drinks, then he looked from her to me slowly. Quietly, he said, "Y'all ready? We have a couple more people to meet before the end, and the end is near. I won't stop this time 'til it's over."

Chapter 9

"Where are they?" Shaggy Dog asked for the seventh time. It was well after midnight, but Jaxson and the Princess had still not arrived. Zero just rolled his eyes and tried to go back to sleep. It had been a long day, and he was not accustomed to carrying squirming cargo even on short flights.

"Shouldn't they be here by now?" asked Shaggy Dog.

At that very moment, the Princess and Jaxson strolled out of the woods, talking and laughing. Just as he was about to admonish them for making him worry, Shaggy Dog paused. The Princess was smiling, *really* smiling. How long had it been since she had looked that happy? Shaggy Dog's tail started its rhythmic swishing and a small smile crept onto his own face.

"Everything good?" he asked.

"Sorry we're so late," giggled the Princess. "Jaxson wanted to show me—"

"Hey!" exclaimed Jaxson. "That's our secret."

The Princess looked at him, and they both burst out laughing again. The smile on Shaggy Dog's face grew. It was so good to hear her laugh.

"Let's just say Jaxson thought he was going to show me how to catch fireflies," said the Princess, "but he doesn't know what fireflies look like."

The Princess and Jaxson could barely breathe as Jaxson said, "But the fairy was shocked when I snagged her from that bush instead."

"I think you were just as shocked," said the Princess. "You squealed like a startled piglet!"

Even Zero chuckled as Jaxson started making pig noises and flailing his arms around in mock surprise.

"Anyway, we made it," said the Princess after catching her breath. "Oh! How was flying with Zero?"

Shaggy Dog's smile faltered. "I prefer the horse."

The whole group had another good laugh at Shaggy Dog's expense.

"Let's have a look at that paw," said Jaxson, getting serious.

"It's not much to look at. I think it's broken," said Shaggy Dog.

Jaxson pulled the lantern close as he examined Shaggy Dog's paw gingerly. Each time Jaxson applied pressure, Shaggy Dog flinched. Finally, Jaxson stated, "It feels like a clean break, which is lucky for you, friend."

"Doesn't feel too lucky," muttered Shaggy Dog.

Jaxson motioned for Zero to come over. As the dragon placed his head next to Shaggy Dog's side, Jaxson said, "I think we can help. Try to hold still."

Before Shaggy Dog could object, Jaxson grasped his paw gently. All his breath escaped Shaggy Dog's lungs as he felt a jolt. Then a tingling sensation moved from Zero through him, to Jaxson, and back. Finally, Jaxson released his paw and hung his head. Sweat dripped from his brow, and his chest heaved.

"That's all I can do," he said without looking up.

Shaggy Dog tested his paw, and it still hurt. However, he found that it could take his weight, and the pain was subsiding by the second.

"Amazing!" said the Princess.

"Yes, it is. What did you do?" asked a wide-eyed Shaggy Dog. Jaxson picked his head up to look at Shaggy Dog and then the Princess.

"It's hard to explain," replied Jaxson. "I don't fully understand it myself, but Zero and I can fix some things. That's all I know."

"Like magic?" she asked.

"If you want to call it that. It's just something we can do. Zero doesn't understand it either. It just feels natural somehow," Jaxson said with a yawn.

The Princess looked at Shaggy Dog expectantly.

"Is there anything you could do about a curse?" asked Shaggy Dog.

Jaxson looked the Princess in the eye. "Zero and I can fix injuries like cuts and bruises. Shaggy Dog's broken paw is the most extreme thing we have ever helped heal. I don't think we could tackle an illness or a curse. Might cause more harm than good."

He led them into his modest house and showed them a bedroom near its rear. They said their goodnights quickly, and Shaggy Dog was asleep before Jaxson closed the door. The Princess waited until she was sure Shaggy Dog wouldn't stir, and then she reached into her pouch and pulled out a vial of glowing blue liquid that the Helm urged her to grab. It was bitter and made her gag, but she was taking three a day nonetheless. She was afraid it would be four tomorrow. The curse brought fatigue and pain that only the vials were able to hold off. Every day was getting harder.

Bitterly cold wind blew in ominous clouds the next day. Jaxson predicted a snowstorm soon, but it was too early for full winter. Shaggy Dog's paw, although greatly improved, was not ready for travel, so the Princess was pleased when Jaxson told them to stay as long as they liked. That night, after a full meal of salted horse, Jaxson told his story. He was sixteen summers old and had been on his own for two summers. His father departed their valley to locate and help dismantle an evil organization bent on destroying all dragons. The Demon Lizard Death Cult, DLDC as they were known, had almost captured Zero as an egg, which is why Jaxson and Zero now lived such an isolated life. Zero hatched when Jaxson was three summers old, and they had been inseparable ever since.

"You have been all alone for two years?" asked Shaggy Dog.

Jaxson shrugged and glanced at Zero. "Yup, just Zero and me."

"Must be hard," replied the Princess.

"It's not all bad. Zero can hunt for food, and during the summer, I catch fish," said Jaxson. "Dragons don't eat as much as you'd think."

"Speaking of your dragon, how did he get his name?" asked a curious Shaggy Dog.

Jaxson laughed. "That's actually a neat story. Come to think about it, I have never told anyone. You see, dragons hatch already knowing their true names. When we connected shortly after he came out of the shell, he told me his name. I was so little I couldn't pronounce it right. 'Zero' was all I could say. The nickname stuck."

"Ahh, that is so sweet," said the Princess. Through the back window, Shaggy Dog saw Zero roll his eyes, and Jaxson made a gagging sound. "And you are one of the only people not to be amazed Shaggy Dog can talk."

"Ha. You recovered pretty quickly from seeing a dragon," commented Jaxson.

"I guess. I have read about dragons and giants and goblins," said the Princess quietly. "Never thought I would meet any of them. I've met them all and more recently."

"I haven't asked yet, but since I told my story…"

The Princess glanced at Shaggy Dog, who gave a slight nod. She formally introduced herself and told her story. Jaxson listened intently, and Zero started at the mention of the huge troll. Then he tilted his head, looking at the Princess with new respect.

Just as she wrapped up her story, there was a knock at the door.

"Expecting someone?" asked Shaggy Dog. He motioned for the Princess to move away from the door.

Again, a knock sounded.

"Not at all," said Jaxson. He looked out the window to see Zero staring back at him. "Zero never saw anyone coming either. I'm gonna see who it is."

Jaxson opened the door to reveal a beard. There was a man attached to it, but he was mostly just white and gray beard.

"Could I trouble you for shelter from this dismal weather?" asked the old man with the beard as he looked around the room. "Have pity on an old man."

He shuffled inside without waiting for permission. The Princess saw Zero take flight, probably to scout the area. She did not believe any harm could come from allowing an old man shelter from the elements. Shaggy Dog was not so sure. Something was strange about this old man and his crooked walking stick, but Shaggy Dog could not figure out exactly what it was.

The old man sat in the only good chair with a sigh of relief. Jaxson stared at him, convinced that he knew him, or at least that he should.

"Do you happen to have anything to eat?" asked the old man.

Jaxson scrambled to prepare a plate even before he realized he had done it. In between bites, the old man kept the conversation flowing with idle chatter.

In an attempt to learn more about the evasive old man, Shaggy Dog asked, "And why were you coming from the east?"

"Well, I have business in the east," he replied curtly. "But with all the trouble and unrest, I thought it wise to explore other options."

Shaggy Dog pounced on an opening. "What type of business are you in, sir?"

The old man put aside his empty plate and responded, "Oh, a little of this and that. Right now, I have a mind to search out artifacts of a past age. Good money can be made from the right relics."

There was a twinkle in his eyes and a hint of a smile through his beard.

"There are some ruins to the south that not many people know about. The ones that do give them a wide berth, 'cause they are supposedly haunted," said Jaxson. He was still puzzled over his familiarity with the old man.

"South, you say? That's good, with the north in open rebellion against King Dranger and his puppets, the DLDC. I have no desire to go north without great reason," said the old man.

Jaxson's head jerked up, and he stared at the old man intently.

"Isn't that the group you were talking about earlier?" asked the Princess, addressing Jaxson.

"It is," Jaxson replied. To the old man, he said, "What do you know of them?"

The old man knew a tremendous amount, not just about the DLDC but about everything. He also seemed to like the sound of his own voice. He talked and talked. When asked a question, his answer would fork off in different directions three times. Hours passed, though it seemed like only moments to Jaxson.

When the old man laughed, Jaxson exclaimed, "It's you! You were there when Dad escaped with Zero as an egg. You used to come by all the time... Dreknoxious! Right?"

"Finally. At your service, Jaxson. Now, where is that pesky dragon of yours?" said the old man cheerfully.

"He scouted the area for a while after you showed up. You know, to see if you were alone. He's out back now," said Jaxson, smiling.

"Is your father about?" asked Dreknoxious.

Jaxson's smile slipped. "No. He left to go find the DLDC years ago. He never came back."

Dreknoxious placed a wrinkled hand on his shoulder and squeezed. "Then we shall just have to go to him," he said, winking.

"Really? Alright – we can leave at first light!" said Jaxson.

"Hold now, boy. This weather will keep us here for at least a day or two," said Dreknoxious. "Besides, our dog friend over there needs to let that paw finish healing."

Shaggy Dog, who had been snoozing, looked up and said, "We don't even know where we are going yet."

"He's right," said the Princess. "Our quest is sort of over, or at least the part we were told about. But it feels like it is just beginning."

Dreknoxious smiled. "Some quests never end, or a new one blends with the old in an unbroken river, forever moving towards its end. And some are over before they start. I happen to know a little something about your quest thus far. I ran into the most bubbly witch yesterday, and she told an amazing tale of a Princess and her companion, one Shaggy Dog. That would be you two, correct?"

The Princess nodded, not really surprised that Dreknoxious already knew about her quest. He seemed to know everything.

"You must fill in the details for me," insisted Dreknoxious.

The Princess told her story again. She felt she was getting quite good at reciting it, out of sheer repetition.

After she had concluded, Dreknoxious said, "Remarkable. You have done so well under such adverse circumstances." Then, quietly, so that only she could hear, he added, "And you hide the pain effectively. But not for much longer,

I am afraid. Be prepared. I may have an idea of what you should do next. I will sleep on it, and we can discuss it in the morning."

The Princess bowed her head in respect. "Thank you, sir."

By the next morning, the weather had worsened. The temperature plummeted, and midday brought freezing rain. The Princess asked if snow was making those strange noises she could hear. It turned out it was hail pelting upon the roof. Zero had retreated up the valley to a large cave overlooking the house to stay dry.

Shaggy Dog's paw was almost back to normal. For the most part, the Princess and Jaxson sat with Dreknoxious, firing question after question at him. The Princess wanted to hear about every magical creature in the world. Jaxson sought information and advice about how to take down the DLDC and hopefully find his dad along the way. For his part, Dreknoxious answered all their enquiries patiently, even expanding on many topics, which only fueled the fire for more questions. As the afternoon wore on, the Princess found herself alone with Dreknoxious. Shaggy Dog was snoozing, and Jaxson had taken off to check on Zero while the rain was light.

"Princess, I wish I could break the curse for you, but I cannot," said Dreknoxious. "I believe that in this whole world, only you have that power."

"I know. I think I have always known I would have to face the Goat Head Sorcerer one on one," replied the Princess.

Dreknoxious nodded and sat up straight. "I do think our paths could be intertwined for a time, however."

The Princess looked back without comment.

"I am of the belief your next move should be to travel to the Oracle," said Dreknoxious. The Princess's eyes grew wide. "She is quite real and nothing like the ridiculous stories told about her. Most importantly, I think she can help you with a plan of attack."

"Do you know where she can be found?"

Dreknoxious laughed. "Just like that, huh?" Shaking his head softly, he continued, "I think I might. Last time I saw her, she was up north near Bent Pine."

The Princess's shoulders sagged, and her eyes grew misty. "That is ever farther from home."

"It is. But during a quest, one must go wherever it leads," said Dreknoxious. "Besides, you may get to meet another elf or even see the steam drakes."

"Not that I am ungrateful for all the great friends I have made, as truly I am. I just hurt, and I am so tired," said the Princess.

Jaxson walked back in, soaked to the bone. The Princess went to help him out of his cloak.

Under his breath, Dreknoxious mumbled, "It's almost over now, sweet Princess."

The following day was spent preparing to depart. The Princess cleaned every inch of her armor and suggested Shaggy Dog take a bath. Everyone laughed, Shaggy Dog loudest of all. Jaxson packed two large bags containing all the food and essentials from the house. He produced a clever harness designed to be strapped around Zero's back. Jaxson planned on walking to try and get more information out of Dreknoxious. After a long day's work, the group felt they were ready to depart at first light the following day. At dusk, Shaggy Dog glanced out the window to see Dreknoxious standing next to the biggest bear he had ever seen. Dreknoxious was listening to it intently. Suddenly, he threw his hands in the air and spoke very quickly to the bear. Shaggy Dog was too far away to hear what was said, but it was plain that the old man was agitated. Moments later, Dreknoxious entered the house and settled at the head of the table.

"Is it time to eat?" he asked with a smile.

"Just leave some for breakfast in the morning," said Jaxson. "I don't want to dig in the bags before the sun has even come up."

Shaggy Dog approached the full table and said, "Haven't seen much game in this valley."

"I imagine the sheep and deer can smell Zero," said Jaxson.

"Oh. I was thinking there might be bears or something else," said Shaggy Dog, glancing at Dreknoxious. Dreknoxious did not flinch; he just continued shoving dried meat into his mouth.

"I've never seen one this far up," said Jaxson, his mouth full of winter berries.

Dreknoxious finally spoke up. "Have you decided where you are going, Princess?"

The Princess cast a glance towards Shaggy Dog, then down at the table. "I haven't discussed it with Shaggy Dog yet, but I think we are going north to seek out the Oracle."

Shaggy Dog's mouth hung open, but before he could respond, Jaxson said, "Me and Zero are going north. We can travel together. Dreknoxious, you should come too. Safety in numbers, you know?"

The Princess observed Dreknoxious's sly smile, despite it being partially hidden by his long beard. "I think that is a wonderful idea. I would love to travel with you two young people for a while, if I can keep up that is."

Chapter 10

Goosebumps invaded the Princess's arms as she stepped into the crisp, sunny morning. The rain and wind had gone, leaving a bluebird sky and chilly air. She watched Zero circle above, the harness holding all of their supplies. She approached Shaggy Dog and Jaxson as she checked that her new sword was secure in the sheath. It was so light that sometimes she forgot it was even there. Shaggy Dog thanked Jaxson again for setting his paw right, but fell silent as Dreknoxious exited the house. The old man walked over to them with the assistance of his gnarled staff. With his free hand, he offered a tall glass to Jaxson.

"Take one pull from this and pass it on," Dreknoxious said.

Jaxson tipped the cup back, then said, "That's nice. What is it?"

The Princess took the cup and immediately smelled spring. As she took a gulp, she thought of flowers and sunshine chasing away a chill. "That is lovely."

Dreknoxious took the cup and a swig. Then he placed it on the ground for Shaggy Dog. "Just an elixir I worked up this morning. It will provide strength and endurance. The side benefit is the taste," he said, winking at the Princess.

Shaggy Dog circled the cup. The smell of wild flowers and the soil after a spring rain filled his nostrils. He circled it again and glanced at Drekoxious out of the corner of his eye. The Princess and Jaxson smiled down at him. Finally, he drank the remainder of the elixir. Immediately his tail swished, and he felt eager to start down the trail.

Jaxson led them out of the valley and up the next mountain. The elixir was everything Dreknoxious said it would be. By midday, the group had traveled farther than Jaxson thought they would all day. When the sun slid level to the horizon, Shaggy Dog said, "Let's make camp. Five more days like that, we'll be at Bent Pine sipping something refreshing."

Zero landed nearby, and they set up camp in short order. As Dreknoxious stirred the beans, he asked Jaxson, "Your father leave any indication of his plans?"

Jaxson stared at the fire. "No. He didn't tell me much at all."

Dreknoxious scooped steaming beans onto the platters, and the Princess passed them out. "I can only conceive two probable scenarios that would keep him absent for so long," said Dreknoxious in between bites. "One is that he located the DLDC and successfully infiltrated the organization. Now, he is waiting from within their own ranks to bring them down."

Still, Jaxson stared at the fire. "And the other?"

"Not something that is pleasant to discuss," said Dreknoxious. "Let's talk about something else, something fun. Like magic."

Jaxson and the Princess shared glances. As Jaxson opened his mouth, the Princess said, "I wish someone could magic this curse out of me."

Dreknoxious sighed deeply, and he looked the Princess in the eye. "As far as I know, there is no magic that can counter the Goat Head Sorcerer's curse in one fell swoop. On this world, anyway."

Shaggy Dog rolled his eyes. "So, you know everything there is to know about magic, old man?"

A smile crept onto Dreknoxious's face. "Not at all. Certainly not. Everything... well, that is a lot. The basics of magic, though, certainly."

The Princess and Jaxson begged Dreknoxious to tell them all that he knew. Dreknoxious was still for long moments, then said, "To discuss magic, first we must discuss magic's source. The common understanding is that magic is fueled by the fabric of realms. Stay with me, now. The spirit realm, the physical realm and the abio – the realm in between – are woven together by magical power. A user of magic is really nothing more than a conduit of that power. The elves can wield the magic of both the physical and the spiritual realm. Wizards can use both as well, but rely heavily on the physical realm. Dark magic is strictly from the spirit realm, witch magic strictly from the physical. And finally, there are dragonwizards – or at least, there were in a past age – that funnel the energy of the abio as their source of magic."

Jaxson shook his head quickly at the Princess. Then he said, "Me and Zero can talk to each other in our thoughts. Does that count?"

"Not really. That connection, although rare, is more common than a dragonwizard," said Dreknoxious.

"Dragonwizards are the most powerful wielders of magic, but they flew too high and almost used too much power for the physical world to withstand. It was them that brought about the Blank Years, and their own destruction."

"Being a dragonwizard sounds complicated," said Jaxson. "Think I'll just stick with my bow."

"It's getting late, Princess," said Shaggy Dog. "We should get some sleep."

The next morning, the group broke camp before the sun crested the mountains and set off downhill. The Princess still felt strong from the elixir she drank the previous day and encouraged by the distance they had already travelled.

As they wrapped up their midday meal, Shaggy Dog pointed out that they had seen no signs of the enemy, and yet almost immediately there came a crashing sound from a small stand of spruce trees below them. The Princess pulled out her sword, and Jaxson nocked an arrow in his bow. Out of the trees stepped a giant bear, moving briskly towards them. Shaggy Dog was sure it was the bear Dreknoxious had talked to at the house.

"Hold your arrow, Jaxson," said Dreknoxious. "Raze is a friend."

Dreknoxious separated himself from the group to meet the bear. Again, Shaggy Dog could not understand the words he spoke, but it was plain that Dreknoxious was agitated by what the bear told him.

When he returned to the group, he spoke quickly. "Princess, stay the course. Seek out the Oracle near Bent Pine. Jaxson, I am going to ask you to accompany her until I return. With luck, I will beat you all there."

"Where are you going?" asked Jaxson.

Dreknoxious, already walking west, said over his shoulder, "Things are escalating quickly. I have urgent business to the west. Stay the course and do not waver!"

He then disappeared into the trees, following the bear.

"What was that about?" asked the Princess.

"I have no idea, but the same bear was at the house talking with Dreknoxious a few days back," said Shaggy Dog. "I'm starting to think there is more to this old man than I first assumed."

"He disappeared awful quick," said Jaxson as he started walking in the direction Dreknoxious had taken. He followed his tracks several steps past the first tree, but then the trail was gone like Drekoxious had simply vanished. *Disappeared is right*, thought Jaxson as he walked back to the Princess and Shaggy Dog.

Even with the elixir wearing off, the group made good time after coming off the mountain. The ground was flat and only with sparse patches of trees.

Two days of travel later, Zero let Jaxson know there was movement in the trees to the west. Whatever it was, it was traveling parallel to them. Each time Zero tried to get a closer look, it would disappear into the thicker trees.

Close to dusk the same day, Shaggy Dog heard the cawing of the Ravens of Despair. Zero launched into the air and drove them back. The group was on high alert that night, so it was little surprise when, shortly before daylight, they heard wolves howling behind them. Shaggy Dog noted how familiar it felt to be harassed by the ravens and to hear the wolves calling to each other. The wolves did not get any closer, but going back to sleep was not an option. After daybreak, the Princess could see that the trees were thinning ahead. Jaxson told the group that Zero could see groups of goblins and large cats with riders in the distance. Still, they were closer to Bent Pine and the Oracle.

"Should only be half a day out of Bent Pine now," said Shaggy Dog at their midday meal. "Maybe we should cut today's travel short."

"Why? We are so close!" said the Princess.

"Yeah, that seems crazy," added Jaxson.

"Just don't think it wise to barrel into a place we aren't familiar with, at dusk," Shaggy Dog said. "We don't know what's waiting for us."

The Princess opened her mouth to protest, but then stopped to listen. Battle horns blared to the west. A few seconds later, a reply echoed from the north.

"Princess, Zero says someone is approaching from the south," said Jaxson, turning to look in that direction.

The Princess loosened her sword in its sheath.

"Who is it?" asked Shaggy Dog.

"He doesn't know, but he says they are struggling past the wolves to get to us," said Jaxson.

Finally, the Princess saw the Benevolent Witch laboring on their trail, huffing and puffing. The Benevolent Witch was almost on top of them before she noticed.

"Oh my!" she exclaimed between ragged breaths. "Finally... caught you."

The Princess smiled and indicated Jaxson. "Hello! This is—"

"No time, Princess, no time," said the Benevolent Witch. She stood up straight. "Dreknoxious sent me to find you."

"Dreknoxious? Where is he? Is he coming back? When?" asked Jaxson rapidly.

The Benevolent Witch's eyes fluttered as she responded, "Yes, yes of course. I am just to deliver a message before he arrives."

She hesitated, looking from Jaxson to the Princess to Shaggy Dog, then back to the Princess.

"Well?" said Shaggy Dog to the Benevolent Witch. "Deliver it, then. We need to decide if we are continuing on or camping here."

The Benevolent Witch's body tensed but her face went slack. She looked at the Princess and said, "The armies of the Goat Head Sorcerer are amassed against you, just a few hours walk from here. Seeking out the Oracle is no longer an option."

"What are we going to do?" asked the Princess, addressing no one in particular.

"There is a simple solution. We turn around and go south. Maybe even home," said Shaggy Dog.

"Zero says we are loosely surrounded. But if we hurry, we can slip through," said Jaxson.

The Benevolent Witch sighed and offered a weak smile. "That may be for the best."

"Jaxson, tell Zero to scout for the best route past them. Then he needs to fly north a ways," said Shaggy Dog. "The enemy will see him and think we're still moving north."

"Wait." The Princess fiddled with her sword's handle as she bit her lower lip.

After long moments, Shaggy Dog said, "Princess, we need to hurry."

"Wait," she said again, pulling out the glass sword. She thought back to all that had happened, from the initial curse to Houstonia to meeting friends and fighting goblins. She thought about finding her sword and meeting a dragon, Zero. "Faith," she muttered. Then more loudly, "Stay the course."

"Princess, we need to escape!" roared Shaggy Dog.

"Zero says we need to leave now," said Jaxson.

"Jaxson, you and Zero should go. Benevolent Witch, you too. Shaggy Dog, I won't insult you by asking you to leave, but I am moving onward," said the Princess. "I am staying the course."

"Of course I am staying with you," said Shaggy Dog gruffly.

"We are too," said Jaxson.

Tears filled the Benevolent Witch's eyes as she nodded.

"Shaggy Dog, find us a place to rest," said the Princess. "Tomorrow, we will stay the course with faith."

The group stumbled through a clump of trees only to encounter a lively campsite. Seven or eight men were dancing to a lute and a stew simmered over the fire. Immediately, Shaggy Dog growled and placed himself in front of the Princess. One of the men stepped forward and greeted them. The Princess could not stifle a smile as she exclaimed "Reserio! Well met. What are you doing here?"

"Obviously, I am dancing a jig," he said. "Come, join us."

The Princess danced and sang. Jaxson hummed along to some of the more popular tunes. Even Shaggy Dog seemed to enjoy himself, though mostly when he was lapping up the delicious stew. Everyone smiled and danced and ate and laughed. No one wanted the evening to end.

Eventually, the revelry faded slowly, as full stomachs led to heavy eyelids. The Princess leaned on Shaggy Dog, and Zero curled around Jaxson. All was perfectly quiet.

"Princess, do you know someone named Sasha?" asked Jaxson suddenly.

"I do," replied the Princess. "Surely I told you about the elf we met. Why do you ask?"

"Well, Zero says she is about to walk into our camp. She just told him so," said Jaxson. "Evidently, she can talk to dragons too."

"Is she? When?" asked the Princess in excitement, standing up.

"Right now," came a voice from the edge of the campfire's ring of light. Sasha and seven other elves stepped into the camp.

"Oh! Sasha! I never thought I'd see you again!" exclaimed the Princess.

Reserio ambled over to see what all the excitement was about.

"How did you find us? Why were you even looking?" asked the Princess as she studied the other elves standing alongside Sasha.

Sasha smiled and said, "Dreknoxious told us what you are up against. I'm not prepared to let you face that alone. I am sad to report that Dane is probably on the other side, though."

"Oh, I was hoping he was with you," said Shaggy Dog. "But it's great to see you nonetheless."

Reserio cleared his throat. "Dreknoxious came to Houstonia and informed us of your situation as well. He even helped us get here."

"And when did he do all this?" asked the Princess.

Reserio and Sasha exchanged glances.

Sasha said, "He appeared to me in a dream four nights ago."

Reserio added, "He was in Houstonia four days ago."

The Princess looked back and forth between them. Appeared in her dream? In Houstonia four days ago? Impossible. Finally, she asked, "Who is he? Really, I mean."

Sasha thought for a moment, then said, "It is not my place to tell anyone."

Jaxson spoke up, "He's not just an eccentric old man, is he?"

Reserio and Sasha both laughed.

"Definitely old, but he is way more than a man. With him on our side, we may defeat the Goat Head Sorcerer yet," answered Reserio.

The Princess yawned despite all the excitement. "I'm getting sleepy," she announced.

"We all should rest," said Reserio. "But first, could I offer a prayer?"

"Of course," replied the Princess.

Reserio moved close to the fire and lifted his left hand and closed his eyes. The only sound was the crackling of the logs. He bowed his head and prayed aloud:

"Let us laugh until we cannot.
Let us love even when we cannot.
Let us be strong until we cannot.
Let us have faith even when we cannot.
Gods, we beseech you,
Let us LIVE until we cannot."

"Well said, witch," Shaggy Dog mumbled. "Well said."

The next morning came quickly. The Princess saw the soft glow above the mountains as she approached the sitting Shaggy Dog. In silence, they watched the sun rise into the sky. Peace before the frenzy.

"I just have to ask, Princess," said Shaggy Dog, "are you sure this is the time to make your stand?"

The Princess uttered a single word: "Yes."

Shaggy Dog stood and faced her. "Stay the course. And I'll be with you. Let's go defeat a sorcerer."

"Let's go," said the Princess with a smile. She looked again at the rising sun and saw a twinkle flash by. "Hey! That looked like a fairy. I miss Jazzi."

Shaggy Dog chuckled. "I liked that jittery little fairy."

Then he too saw a flash, and then another. Soon there were flashes all around them. Jazzi landed lightly on Shaggy Dog's snout and curtsied.

"Well, I'll be," said Shaggy Dog. Jazzi's hands moved around very fast, then she flew to the Princess. Gently, she kissed her cheek and buzzed off to join the other fairies.

"She and her whole family have been here all night," said Shaggy Dog. "The Ravens of Despair tried to sneak into camp six times, but the fairies fended them off. Jazzi says she'll meet us on the field."

"She looks so happy to be back with her family," said the Princess.

A battle horn blared to the east. It was answered from the north by three different horns.

"Time to see what we're up against," said the Princess as she turned back to the camp.

Minutes later, the Princess and Shaggy Dog were on the march. Sasha and the other elves scouted ahead. The Princess saw glimpses of the fairies darting in and out of the trees, and Jaxson on Zero's back circled above. The Benevolent Witch, Reserio, and the witches of Houstonia followed, providing a rear guard. They marched towards the horns. They marched to danger and to the Goat Head Sorcerer.

Ravens of Despair circled above and to the left. A multitude of steam drakes, each about twice the size of an eagle with a serpentine body and thin wings, circled above and to the right. Directly across the field, at the base of a gentle hill, stood a wall of goblins and trolls. gathered behind them were the Snake Oil Witches and the giants. Another wall of goblins separated the lizard knights on their feline mounts from the rest of the army.

On top of the hill, standing tall and still, the Goat Head Sorcerer surveyed his army. To his left, wolves patrolled the mountain passes. He would not allow surprises nor escape from the battle.

The Princess felt despair bloom in her chest. She had no idea what she had been expecting, but this many against her was certainly not it. Shaggy Dog glanced at her, then back at the field.

The group came to a halt with the witches of Houstonia and the elves in front. Jaxson and Zero patrolled the sky above. Jazzi and her family of fairies remained to the left. The Benevolent Witch stood beside the Princess with her mouth hanging open.

"Princess, I feel sorry for them," Shaggy Dog said, indicating the enemy army.

The Princess smirked. "And why is that?"

"They didn't bring any reinforcements," said Shaggy Dog. "They are in a heap of trouble."

The Princess laughed and loosened her sword in the scabbard.

She jumped when a battle horn sounded directly behind them. Before anyone could react, two platoons of mounted knights streamed out of the forest, led by Sergeant Rivers. They moved to the front of the line and assembled alongside the others. The Queen came out next to stand beside the Princess. She bowed her head slightly, and the Princess gave a formal bow in return. Tears streamed down the Princess's face as she scanned all around, looking for Dreknoxious. He was nowhere to be found.

This was her army, outnumbered and outmatched, but all were willing to battle for her.

Battle horns blared from the enemy side. The first line of goblins and trolls parted to allow the giants to move forward. The Princess's heart sank to her toes. On the front lines stood Dane, carrying a menacing cudgel. A giant in the middle started beating a drum, and the group advanced slowly. As the drumming increased, the giants gained speed. The ground shook, and the Princess's armor rattled.

A battle cry from Dane split the air, and suddenly the giants stopped halfway between the opposing forces. Dane turned to face his brethren. More than half the giants started walking off the field. The remainder followed Dane slowly to the line of the Queen's knights.

"Shagg Doog!" thundered Dane. "Dane help Princess!"

Shaggy Dog's tail swished violently side to side as he weaved to the front lines. The Princess smiled at the Benevolent Witch's puzzled expression.

"He's a friend," the Princess said.

"I see," the Benevolent Witch replied.

They both watched as Shaggy Dog issued commands to the knights, then went out to greet Dane. The giants turned in the opposite direction, and as one bellowed a challenge at the armies of the Goat Head Sorcerer.

The sorcerer laughed loudly. Then, with a flick of his hand, the first wave of goblins and trolls attacked.

The Ravens of Despair swooped towards the Princess's army, and the Snake Oil Witches readied glass jars filled with burning liquid to hurl. The Princess closed her eyes and whispered Reserio's prayer from the previous night. When she opened her eyes again, she pulled the glass sword from its scabbard.

Dane and the giants sprang towards the advancing horde. Jazzi and the fairies flew to intercept the ravens. Just before the clash, the Snake Oil Witches threw the evil jars of liquid fire towards the giants. Reserio and the witches of Houstonia were ready. Before the jars could shatter against the giants, the witches propelled them towards the goblins using magic. Reserio gave the Princess and Shaggy Dog a wink. The jars exploded, sending foul liquid into the lines of goblins. Many fell screeching, and then the giants were among them. Dane and his brethren were behemoths on the battlefield, and not a single goblin nor troll within the first wave survived. The giants pulled back, waiting for the next attack as Jazzi and the fairies chased the ravens into the mountains.

The Princess's confidence swelled. The enemy's armies had taken grave losses, and yet all of her friends remained uninjured. She watched as the Snake Oil Witches scrambled to get behind the next line of goblins, then she smiled as she surveyed the field. Her eyes locked onto the Goat Head Sorcerer. He clapped softly, and her smile faltered.

Then the remainder of the goblins and trolls attacked. Dane and the giants, along with the witches of Houstonia, met them in the middle of the field. Jaxson and Zero swooped down to take out a particularly nasty troll. Before they could ascend back to the skies, the steam drakes attacked en masse. There were so many! Jaxson flung arrow after arrow, striking a drake almost every time, but still there were more. Zero took to the sky and circled, but the drakes persisted. Zero's left wing was gashed and blood oozed from a cut on his back leg. Jaxson only had a few arrows left. He put one to his bowstring, pulled it back, and aimed carefully from Zero's back. As soon as he released the string, he knew the arrow was on target.

The second before it struck the heart of the Goat Head Sorcerer, a pulse shot out from his chest. The arrow shattered in midair. Zero struggled to stay in the air after reeling from the pulse, so Jaxson nudged him towards the safety of the mountains.

The strange lizard knights on their big cats joined the fray. Sasha and the elves met them eagerly, but the lizard knights were very fast. The tide was turning in favor of the enemy army.

Shaggy Dog looked at the Princess, and she smiled.

"It's time, little one," he said gently.

"Stay the course," she responded, then raised her sword and shouted a battle cry.

The Princess's army, emboldened by her courage, fought even harder. The Queen's knights helped the elves drive off the lizard knights. The giants and witches of Houstonia attacked the remaining goblins. The Princess, followed closely by Shaggy Dog and the Benevolent Witch, shot into the battle like an arrow. The fighting was intense, but the Princess and Shaggy Dog cut and bit any minion of the vile sorcerer unlucky enough to get close.

Then the Princess heard Reserio yell, "They are on the run! Advance!"

The giants followed Dane and Reserio, pushing the goblins back. The Princess's army was winning.

Then a terrible thunder erupted. The Goat Head Sorcerer descended from the hill and strode towards the Princess. He waved his hand, producing magic to freeze Shaggy Dog and the Benevolent Witch in place. He uttered a spell and a wall of rock shot up between the Princess and her army.

He towered above her and laughed. "All alone now, Princess," he said. "Just you and me."

The Princess looked at her sword, then met his gaze without flinching. "I will stay the course. I will LIVE without fear! I will live until I cannot," she screamed as she leveled her sword and attacked.

Despite his large size, the Goat Head Sorcerer sidestepped the charging Princess quickly and placed a boot on her back. She flew to the ground, hard. As she struggled to rise, the Goat Head Sorcerer tossed aside his serrated sword and laughed.

Again, she charged, taking the fight to him, and again the Goat Head Sorcerer sidestepped and laughed.

"Fight me!" she screamed.

"In good time," replied the Goat Head Sorcerer. He began to circle the Princess slowly. She lashed out with Faith, but the Goat Head Sorcerer danced away. "I thought when Dane the Giant volunteered to lead the charge, he was eager to show his loyalty. I was wrong about that."

The Princess slashed again and said, "You are wrong about many things."

The Goat Head Sorcerer cackled and reached down for his sword. The Helm of Knowledge urged the Princess to quickly search her pack for a vial of Dragon's Fire. Before the sorcerer was upright, the Princess drank it down, and the Goat Head Sorcerer was greeted with flames directly in his face. He stumbled, one arm, his neck and his face smoldering. The Princess fell to one knee, but she was happy to see her gamble had wounded the sorcerer. He bellowed with rage, and the Princess barely had time to stand before she was attacked. She danced back, blocking and avoiding every thrust and jab he threw at her.

"Neat trick with the fire, but it's over, little girl," jeered the Goat Head Sorcerer.

"Not yet!" screamed the Princess and resumed the attack. She feinted low, then struck high, hoping the sorcerer's wounded shoulder would prevent him from blocking.

The sorcerer parried and stepped to one side, bringing his sword around and landing a bone-rattling strike to the center of her chest. The Princess flew fifteen feet to land in a heap of her own armor. The Helm of Knowledge flew off and her breastplate cracked.

The Goat Head Sorcerer stalked towards her.

Suddenly, the Princess heard a victorious cry from her army.

"We will never stop. I will never stop, and they will never stop fighting you," the Princess said from the ground.

The sorcerer looked in the direction of the triumphant cries and started an incantation. When he closed his eyes and raised his arms, the Princess drank another vial and covered him with searing flame. He let out a bloodcurdling scream and released his unused power.

The world grew fuzzy for the Princess as she tumbled away. The next thing she knew, she was staring into the blue, cloudless sky.

The Goat Head Sorcerer approached, steaming and with one horn broken off. He raised his sword for the final blow.

The Princess's defiant scream rang out as she pushed Faith up to block the attack.

The glass sword shattered on impact, so that only the thin, silver core remained. The sorcerer kicked her in the ribs, the damaged breastplate providing inadequate protection. The Princess struggled but could not rise to her feet. Every breath was agony, and her head throbbed.

The Goat Head Sorcerer raised his weapon and said, "I curse you."

A red shadow passed over the battlefield. The Princess smiled as she looked up. The sorcerer hesitated and looked to the sky. A red dragon twice the size of Zero swooped overhead. It turned and came straight towards them.

Dreknoxious was on the back of the dragon, grasping his staff – except the staff was not gnarled wood; instead, it was golden, smooth and straight. The old man jumped from the dragon and landed gracefully beside the Princess. The Goat Head Sorcerer watched the dragon wheel and fly over the mountains before he turned his attention to the newcomer.

"You have no authority or power here, wizard," hissed the Goat Head Sorcerer.

"The battle is over," said Dreknoxious sternly.

The sorcerer, still smoking from the Dragon's Fire, laughed loudly. "You are right about that. She is mine!"

Dreknoxious placed his shimmering staff into the ground and muttered a series of strange words. Then he looked at the Goat Head Sorcerer and said, "You are finished here today."

There was a soft click, and then the Goat Head Sorcerer was gone.

The wall separating the Princess from the army fell away. The Benevolent Witch and Shaggy Dog, freed from the freezing spell, ran to the Princess's side. Dreknoxious lowered his head and mumbled to himself, and then his golden staff changed back into the twisted, old wooden walking stick as he shuffled over to the Princess.

"Is she alright?" asked a panicked Shaggy Dog.

"She is still breathing," said the Benevolent Witch. "Beyond that, I am unsure."

The Queen hurried over and asked what had happened. Dane and Reserio approached, followed quickly by Sasha and Jazzi.

"Give her some room," said Dreknoxious. "Go and tend to your wounded. Benevolent Witch, if you please?"

"Yes, right away," she said. She pulled her wand from inside her traveling cloak and waved it.

A large tent materialized around them. Once her broken armor was removed, they placed the Princess on a comfortable pallet. Reserio found the Helm of Knowledge, brought it to the tent, and laid it at her feet beside the remnants of Faith and the shattered Armor of Love.

The Princess breathed softly, surrounded by Shaggy Dog, the Benevolent Witch, Dreknoxious, and the Queen. Her eyes fluttered open. Shaggy Dog was at her side in an instant. Tears spilled from his eyes as he licked the dirt and blood off the Princess's face.

"I thought I had lost you," he whispered.

"Not yet," said the Princess weakly.

"Just rest, little one," said Shaggy Dog.

"I'm not sure rest will help," she said.

"Here, drink some water," offered the Benevolent Witch. "Slowly now. Do you feel up to eating something?"

The Princess shook her head. Dreknoxious came forward and placed a hand on the Princess's forehead. The interior of the tent was eerily still.

The Princess looked into the eyes of the old man that was more than a man and muttered, "Thank you."

Then, loud enough for everyone to hear, she said, "Thank you all."

"You hurt him, Princess. You hurt him bad," said Shaggy Dog. The Princess only nodded, so he continued, "I think we should press him while he is injured. Not this second, of course, but very soon. We need to capitalize on this victory."

"Hush now, you silly dog," said the Benevolent Witch. "The Princess is severely injured. We should seek out the healers of Ranah. Let's get her strong again before we thrust her so quickly into another battle."

"The time to rest has escaped us. We have come too far and sacrificed too much. She has sacrificed too much to stop now," screamed Shaggy Dog.

"We can't go on right now," said the Benevolent Witch loudly. "She needs to rest!"

Shaggy Dog's eyes were on fire as he stared at the Benevolent Witch. "I have been with her the entire way. She is stronger than anyone will ever know."

The two bickered back and forth for long minutes, neither conceding to the other. Dreknoxious was about to intervene when the Princess cleared her throat softly. All eyes turned to her as she said, "I'm not sure what is best. But I don't know that I can fight anymore."

Shaggy Dog wilted and the hardness in his eyes evaporated. "Oh, little one."

"I am so sorry," whispered the Princess.

"Don't apologize to me or anyone else, not ever. You have nothing to be sorry for," he said.

Just beyond the foot of the pallet, near the shattered sword, a shaft of light appeared. The Princess was the only one that did not shield her eyes against its brilliance. From inside the light, music flowed as a form appeared. Out stepped a little man the Princess recognized immediately.

"Peddler? I have even less to trade this time," she said.

"I have played many parts before, and you have seen me as a peddler. Not tonight, though," said Mikaela as he spread a pair of angelic wings wide.

The Princess's eyes darted to Dreknoxious as she said, "No one is who they portray themselves to be lately."

The old man had the awareness to appear abashed, lowering his head in acknowledgement. The Queen and the Benevolent Witch each bent a knee and lowered their heads as well.

"Appearances can be deceiving," said Mikaela with a smile. "I think we need a moment."

He snapped his fingers, and the world around them froze. *This is different than the Goat Head Sorcerer's freezing spell*, thought the Princess. *This is more.* She studied her friends for a long time before adjusting her head on the pillow to focus on the angel.

"I know why you are here, and I am so relieved," she said quietly. When Mikaela did not respond, she continued, "But I am also sad. Do I have a choice?"

"There are always choices, child," said Mikaela, spreading his arms wide. The tent filled with sweet voices rising in song, without words. "Some are just easier to make than others."

Everywhere the Princess looked, an angel appeared. There were tall angels and short ones. Some appeared old and others young. They were all beautiful and all were singing the wordless song.

"Do I get to say goodbye?" she asked.

Mikaela thought for a moment. "Certainly. Shaggy Dog is going to take it better than you think; I know you worry for him. He will try to be strong for you. His trial will come later, but I have an idea about that."

He motioned one of the little angels forward. The Princess smiled at the tiny, glowing angel despite her pain. Her smile was matched by the angel.

"Princess, this is Ariana. She has a talent that is quite special. Whenever her family left on this world is in deep sorrow or missing her more than normal, she paints the sky to remind them of the beauty all around them. Would you like her to teach you how?"

Tears streamed down the Princess's face. "I would like that very much."

Mikaela reached down and grasped the handle of Faith. He placed the tip of the silver rod into the ground and pushed the handle down gently. The handle slid down the silver core, and a shining light radiated out from it. Through the light the Princess saw wings unfurling from the silver core. When Mikaela was finished and the light dimmed, a magnificent set of angel's wings had replaced her sword, Faith.

"Are you ready, child?"

"I don't want to hurt anymore. I gave it all I had and kept Faith. I am ready," she replied.

Everyone was moving again. The Princess turned to Shaggy Dog and locked eyes.

"I stayed the course with Faith," she said.

In that moment, Shaggy Dog knew the fight was over. It was not a bolt of new knowledge, but instead an unveiling of the truth that had lingered in his mind for days. He leaned in close and whispered, "You are the bravest person I know, and it is my pleasure to call you my friend. And I will miss you with all my heart, but I don't want you to hurt anymore. You hid it so well, but I knew. Starting in Houstonia, I knew. I saw the pain the curse made you endure, and later the weariness the dragon's fire caused. But I, also, watched you push on anyway. You are so much stronger than me."

"I am strong because of you," she said. "Let me tell you a secret."

Shaggy Dog leaned in even closer as the Princess continued, "There is an angel here with me – you cannot see her, but she is here. Her name is Ariana, and she has the most beautiful smile. She is going to teach me to paint. Isn't that great? Every time you see a brilliant sunset or colorful sunrise with pink and blue, purple, and orange, you will know I am thinking of you."

Shaggy Dog's voice quaked as he whispered to her. "Little one."

The Benevolent Witch and Queen cried softly. Dreknoxious lowered his head.

The Princess looked at Mikaela and said, "I am ready."

At that moment, everyone in the tent with the Princess, and those outside waiting, heard the voices of the angels sing their wordless song. Shaggy Dog laid beside the Princess for a long time even as she was testing her new wings, and he cried. He cried because she felt no more pain, and he cried because he missed her already. He cried.

Chapter 11

The wetness on my cheeks spilled onto the bar. I saw the little splash as a tear made contact with the old wood. The only sounds in the room were deep breathing from Daniel and quiet sobs from Brandee. The fire was gone from Daniel's eyes. His face seemed to have smoothed, having become more gentle in the last few minutes. The deep lines and the scowl had disappeared, revealing a much younger man than I had first assumed.

"That's the story I told Josie, my princess, as she lay in the hospital bed," he said into the still bar.

"I'm so sorry," was all I managed to reply.

Daniel rose from his stool and started for the exit. Without a thought, I fell in step, with Brandee right behind me. The sound of waves crashing politely into the sandy beaches greeted us as we stepped into the gloomy, predawn morning. Birds were just beginning to summon the sun from its slumber as we paused and looked out over the sea. I stood beside Daniel as he gazed across the water.

The fiery red sun was rising through clouds of orange and pink. The sky framed it with a backdrop of light purple flowing to midnight blue. I had never seen a more beautiful sight in all my life.

We stood there together, watching the sun rise on a new day, each with our own thoughts. I thought of Janie, and of time wasted, but also of time granted. I decided right then to make a fresh start with her.

After an indiscernible amount of time, Daniel looked at us and then back at the sunrise.

Finally, he said, "My princess turned into one hell of a good painter."

Special Thanks

A special thank you to my wife for wading into the strange waters of dragons, goblins, and talking dogs with me.

Thank you to my kids for loving my story even if there are no dinosaurs or unicorns.

For constant support and encouragement, I want to thank my mother. I did it, Mama.

Thank you to Kennon Barton and Red Basement Publishing for the original cover design.

To the Helen Hall Library Writer's Club, let's keep dreaming on paper together.

And finally, to you the reader, thank you for giving this book your time.

About The Author

C. H. Smith earned a BA in English from Belhaven College in Jackson, MS much to the surprise of faculty. He considers family to be his top priority and friends to be family. He is a son, a brother, an uncle, a husband, and a father. He also likes to write stories.

Books By This Author

Nothing More than Zero

A YA fantasy adventure full of magic, danger, and discovery. The portals linking the world are all but forgotten. The ancient line of Dragon Kings are passed beyond myth. But a boy and his dragon on a quest to find the boy's missing father revive both.

Encountering powerful enemies, unnatural storms, and ruthless bounty hunters is not exactly how he hoped his search would go. Every move Jaxson makes causes more problems. He will have to rely on the friends he just met, his wits, and most of all his dragon Zero, if he hopes to survive long enough to find his father.

Dangers await them on their quest, but there is no turning back. Jaxson needs to find his father, and Zero needs to find answers about his past. Both are unsure what they will discover, but at least they will find it together.

www.ingramcontent.com/pod-product-compliance
Lightning Source LLC
Chambersburg PA
CBHW020044310726
48970CB00007B/2397